WHERE TO CARRY
THE SOUND

The Year of Perfect Happiness by Becky Adnot-Haynes
Matt Bell, Judge

Last Words of the Holy Ghost by Matt Cashion
Lee K. Abbott, Judge

The Expense of a View by Polly Buckingham
Chris Offutt, Final Judge

ActivAmerica by Meagan Cass
Claire Vaye Watkins, Final Judge

Quantum Convention by Eric Schlich
Dolan Morgan, Final Judge

Orders of Protection by Jenn Hollmeyer
Colin Winnette, Final Judge

Some People Let You Down by Mike Alberti
Zach VandeZande, Final Judge

They Kept Running by Michelle Ross
Polly Buckingham, Final Judge

There Is Only Us by Zoe Ballering
Polly Buckingham, Final Judge

What Did You Do Today? by Anthony Varallo
Molly Giles, Final Judge

WHERE TO CARRY THE SOUND

Stories by
Nina Sudhakar

2024 Winner, Katherine Anne Porter Prize in Short Fiction

University of North Texas Press
Denton, Texas

Printed in the United States of America.

10 9 8 7 6 5 4 3 2 1

Permissions:
University of North Texas Press
1155 Union Circle #311336
Denton, TX 76203-5017

The paper used in this book meets the minimum requirements of the American National Standard for Permanence of Paper for Printed Library Materials, z39.48.1984. Binding materials have been chosen for durability.

Library of Congress Cataloging-in-Publication Data

Names: Sudhakar, Nina, author.
Title: Where to carry the sound / stories by Nina Sudhakar.
Description: Denton, Texas : University of North Texas Press, 2024. |
    Series: Katherine Anne Porter prize in short fiction series ; number 23
Identifiers: LCCN 2024042623 (print) | LCCN 2024042624 (ebook) |
    ISBN 9781574419498 (paperback) | ISBN 9781574419580 (ebook)
Subjects: BISAC: FICTION / Short Stories (single author) | LCGFT: Short stories.
Classification: LCC PS3619.U348 W47 2024 (print) | LCC PS3619.U348 (ebook) |
    DDC 813/.6--dc23/eng/20240923
LC record available at https://lccn.loc.gov/2024042623
LC ebook record available at https://lccn.loc.gov/2024042624

Where to Carry the Sound is Number 23 in the Katherine Anne Porter Prize in Short Fiction series.

The electronic edition of this book was made possible by the support of the Vick Family Foundation.

CONTENTS

CONTENTS

Acknowledgments

So many people, places, and experiences were instrumental in the creation of this work. I would like to express my immense gratitude to the following: To Ron Chrisman, Amy Maddox, and everyone at UNT Press for bringing this book to life. To Molly Giles for selecting this work for this unbelievable honor. To all the readers, editors, and staff of the publications where some of these stories first appeared for seeing something in these words and helping these stories find their final forms. To Aleesha Nandhra for the amazing cover art. To my cohorts and faculty at Pink Door, Tin House, and Kenyon, and my writing group in Chicago; I am a better writer for having been in your company. To all tellers of myth, legend, undertold histories, and folklore (including A. K. Ramanujan, whose retelling of "The Dead Prince and the Talking Doll"—and of course, Sei Shōnagon's *The Pillow Book*— inspired "Pillow Book of the Dead Prince's Intended") for preserving those stories. To all the public libraries and independent bookstores I've frequented for a world I felt I belonged in—one built of writers, readers, and books.

To an all-star constellation of childcare workers, teachers, and helping hands for pockets of time that could be emptied onto these and other pages.

To my parents and my grandparents, without whom neither I nor these stories would exist, who first nurtured a belief that my stories were worth telling. To my parents-in-law for loving care and support. To my brother and all my brothers- and sisters-in-law for laughter and camaraderie. To them and all the rest of my family (by birth, by marriage, by friendship, the whole sprawling bunch assembled by so many means): you are who I love, and I am so grateful to be a part of your community.

To Siggi for companionship. To Daniel for everything; this dream grew wings because of you. To Rowan and Ash for altering my perspective; my world is filled with so much joy, wonder, and magic because you are in it. May you grow to greet a world more radically beautiful than our wildest individual imaginings.

And to you, dear reader, for the life this book will live in your hands.

Come Tomorrow

Every house in the village looked identical, which made it difficult for Diya to decide where to knock for help. In the absence of any distinguishing features—a worn jute welcome mat, cane rocking chairs on the front porch, a pink tricycle beached on its side out front—she had no means by which to form a snap impression as to who behind each closed door might be warm, hospitable, safe. She'd bitten her tongue when the front tire on the scooter she'd been driving reached its final stage of deflation. Her entire morning's journey had been accompanied by its quiet hiss, especially when she passed the outermost suburbs, and vehicles, humans, and animals became more scarce, just palms and dried-up streams and bugs flying into her helmet's visor to keep her company. She could still taste the blood in her mouth— fresh, metallic, signaling *emergency*.

Behind her she could hear a cluster of desiccated palms rustling, their trunks stooped as if broken, finally, by a lack of water, of care. Diya felt like the only living creature for miles. On first—even second or third—glance the village seemed not an inhabited community but a small assemblage of abandoned buildings, several homes arrayed on lanes shooting off from the main road that carried most people to and from elsewhere.

Diya, too, had been on her way elsewhere, about half an hour farther down the road to an NGO that provided employment for women skilled in a near-extinct form of embroidery. One of the organization's international donors had arranged a professional photoshoot for their new website, which Diya had been hired to conduct according to very specific instructions: meticulously posed *candids* of the women at work; macro-zoomed shots of fabric tight enough to see every careful stitch; hands; needles; mirrorwork; cowrie shells; spools of thread. The donor representative she'd been in contact with kept calling the women's work a *dying art*, as if the women weren't alive and practicing it. Diya could read between the lines. Her task was to produce images from a future in which the work had already died and then been *miraculously resurrected*.

Diya suspected, perhaps, that she'd been contacted for the job on the basis of an interview she'd done recently with the curator of an email newsletter focused on various creatives' processes. The curator's first question, delivered without any preamble, was: what is/are your preoccupation(s)? Though Diya understood the intention behind the question, its value, it felt intrusive, like a demand to enter the sheltered space of the innermost room of her brain, a request to publish her unfiltered internet search history from the past year. She allowed as much silence to pass as seemed socially acceptable before deciding to tell the truth.

My primary motivation, she told the curator, *is to capture the ineffable. Perhaps my only distinct memory of my mother is from when I must have been around five; when she'd flip the light switch off at bedtime and I balked at the darkness, she'd tell me not to worry because I was never alone, there were always ghosts all around me. "Just look," she said, "you'll see them, and you can tell me about them." And I did look, and it took awhile, but I did see them everywhere, often not in the forms I would have expected. Ghost as presence, not absence, right? A material remnant. What inhabits the space, not what's lost from it. So I'm not interested in the double exposure, really, but rather the single image that represents both realities, simultaneously death and rebirth . . .* Here Diya had trailed off, stricken at having revealed so much, and tacked on the added hedge, . . . *if that makes sense.*

When the interview was published, she saw that she'd missed a note somewhere about her answers being condensed for inbox digestibility and attention spans. What were her preoccupations? A short, bulleted list:

- ghosts
- mothers
- materials
- the multiverse
- reincarnation

❧

The tire's final gasp had occurred several hundred yards from the village. Diya checked her phone again, fruitlessly, knowing the battery remained dead. The few shops lining the main road were closed, though it was still early afternoon and a season of pleasant weather, not yet hot or rainy or both. Behind the road was a large, empty square that might have known green grass at some point but now boasted only a few yellowed clumps.

In thirty minutes Diya had managed to walk the length of every lane, feeling increasing dread as she did so. All of the houses were built in an old style once typical in the area, now likely to be called *heritage* in tourist brochures: large, one-story structures formed from whitewashed brick with wooden pillars supporting an overhanging red-tiled roof. Inside, Diya knew, the houses' rooms would face an open-air courtyard. There was no deviation in the architecture or exterior decoration of the houses in the village; they appeared to her as if they had all been erected by the same builder at the exact same time, carbon copies that had somehow managed even to age at the same rate. The phrase *arrested decay* popped into her mind, which she'd learned during a previous project photographing historic buildings that local authorities had agreed to maintain only to the extent that they wouldn't be allowed to collapse.

There was a small patch of bare land in front of each house, but nothing had been planted there, no clotheslines strung up or animals wandering around, no remnants of flowers blown out of garlands from previous auspicious days, no outward signs that any house was inhabited. Yet the place also had the feeling of one only recently vacated, the air charged and unsettled like in a room a person has just exited. Like everyone there had seen her coming and immediately retreated, seeking not just invisibility but removal from this plane of existence.

As Diya made a second loop, looking more closely at the houses, she noticed that above each weathered teak door was a word or words in the same script. She recognized the looped strings of characters as her (grand)mother's language, remembering the way she'd always thought the script matched the soft, rounded vowels of the words spoken aloud when she'd overheard them, rarely. The way some curved letters, to her wholly untrained eye, appeared just like her grandmother's cupid-bowed lips forming the sound *ooooo.*

Initially, Diya had taken the writing above each door as the family name of each house's residents, a single nod to individuality amid the jarring homogeneity. But as she completed her second pass, she felt confident that all of the writing spelled exactly the same word or phrase. Perhaps the name of the village, she thought. Or maybe one large, extended family had settled in this place, and each house bore that same name.

She made a third pass through the lanes, this time knocking on each house's door. The doors were more solid than they looked, thick slabs of wood that seemed to absorb all sound. A few times she thought she detected rustling fabric, the slap of a sandal. But no person came to open the door, and this seemed so unfathomable, given what she now knew of the local culture, having immersed herself for some time in her (grand) mother's city, in the constant desire to know another person's business, the almost overbearing hospitality, that she began to doubt she'd heard anything. It seemed impossible that there were people within each of these houses listening to her and feeling no compulsion to even open a window and peek out at the woman making all this noise.

The sun was now tracing the lower half of its arc toward the horizon. Diya had walked around the side of the last house in the last lane and was standing beside a curtained window. She covered her face with her hands, feeling the sweat and road grit that coated it. It was easier to think with her eyes closed, in that darkness. She pressed her eyes with her fingertips until she saw sparks.

She'd go back to the road, she thought. Wait for a vehicle to pass or start walking until she came to another village.

She sensed the wind picking up, whistling through the dried palm leaves. But no—not the wind, which could not form words—for as she listened closer Diya realized she could make out murmured words, the cadence of chanting, coming from behind the window. Someone inside, whispering what sounded like a prayer.

Hello, she called out, is someone there? My scooter broke down and I'm stuck. Please, can you help me?

The whispering behind the window stopped. The silence filled the sound's absence.

I know there's someone there, Diya said. I heard you. Please, can you help me?

After a pause, Diya heard a woman's voice. Go away, it said. It sounded less like a command and more like an entreaty.

Leave me be, please, the voice continued. I cannot help you.

Diya felt her skin prickle with anxiety, her breath quicken with the beginnings of desperation. The only person she'd located did not have any interest in helping her.

The curtain shifted and Diya could make out a single fearful eye peering at her, still standing there, not having left. She held up her hands, a gesture of surrender.

Please, Diya said, I'm not here to hurt you.

Another long pause and then the curtain was drawn back, revealing a woman with a navy-blue shawl draped over her head and held over her face. From her hands and the slight bend to her back, Diya could tell the woman was elderly but couldn't discern any features or facial expression. Diya could make out a bed and almirah in the room behind her, a family portrait hanging on the wall to her left.

Look, Diya said, you have a daughter, right? Wouldn't you want someone to help your child if they were stuck somewhere?

The hand holding the woman's shawl to her face dropped to her chest. The woman's hair was almost fully white, but her face bore no lines, no signs of age.

How do you know I have a daughter? The woman's voice was high and pained.

Diya pointed to the portrait.

Yes, the woman said, low and soft, almost to herself. She's a bit older than you but you look a bit like her, you know.

I just need to borrow a phone, Diya said. That's all and then I'll be gone.

The woman cracked open the window enough to pass her cell phone through.

Come around front when you're done, she said, shutting the window. You can leave the phone there.

Diya made her call and then walked to the front door as instructed. As she rounded the corner, she saw that the woman had placed a bottle of water and a plastic plate of stale biscuits on the ground. With the more urgent problem now solved, she remembered her hunger. She ate and drank and then left the woman's phone on the plate.

It had been ill-advised to borrow the scooter; it belonged to an award-winning photojournalist Diya had previously known only in passing. She knew his photographs first, of course, immediately recognizable as his, images so beautifully composed as to seem staged though they were of moments impossible to orchestrate.

She'd read somewhere that he was on assignment in her (grand)mother's city, and soon after her arrival there, on an open-ended whim to freelance but also desperate for company, she'd looked him up and messaged him for a drink. He had just finished an assignment following paranormal researchers into places no one, including the photojournalist, wanted to go. He said the researchers liked to tell of a previous cameraman who'd accompanied them, who had pissed himself after a series of unspeakable events in a decrepit seaside colonial fort. It was intended to be regarded as a great kindness that no one had commented on the puddle accumulating by the man's feet at the time, but left unexamined that they continued to relay the story to others after the fact, years later, and here was the photojournalist now telling it to her.

What brings you to the city? he'd asked, returning her question. Do you have family here or some connection to this place? He was sitting sidesaddle on a barstool and facing her, making sustained eye contact. She felt like a bug ready to burn under a magnifying glass.

No, she said. I was sort of between things so thought I'd spend some time here, try to pick up a few jobs. Diya didn't say that the things she was between were her grandmother's death and whatever lay beyond, more stages of grief and a future she'd never, even prior to her life's accumulating losses, envisioned clearly. That she thought simply being in this place, long ago relinquished by her grandmother and mother, might spur the kind of revelation that gave a life purpose.

Yeah, the photojournalist said, I get that. It's tough cobbling things together. I always hated having to line things up all the time. Diya gathered from his slight smile as he said this that he was self-aware about his current professional status, which involved others chasing him rather than the other way around.

Why photography? he asked. What got you into it?

The box of family photographs under my bed, Diya thought—the way she'd grown up thumbing through the stack, envying the way an image could capture, could hold a person in place. The wooden toy camera in that same box, which her mother had picked up in this city and given to Diya as a baby, the only toy Diya had saved from childhood. It had no functionality other than to look like a camera, but it didn't feel like a useless object; the symbolism felt weighty, like her mother had meant it to tell her something. On the back, a pair of eyes were painted along with a line in the local script. Underneath, her mother had written in English, *What do you see?*

It kind of fell into my lap when I was younger, Diya said, and the photojournalist accepted this, moving on to another subject.

In one of their first meetings Diya had asked him, *What's your best ghost story?* and this had developed into a game between them, both of them trading stories, the stories eventually evolving into masks, feints, secrets, like two truths and a lie, some real kernel buried among the other realities they'd chosen to label as fiction.

Once, a person:

(*a*) *drowned in a pothole and now emerges from the pitted street after every rainfall, luring drivers to their demise.*

(*b*) *died of old age and decided to check in on how their descendants were doing, a hundred years later.*

(*c*) *lost their newborn to disease while a doctor was out drinking, and returns to the town posing as a stranger seeking aid in order to gain entry to the residents' houses and steal their children.*

(*d*) *set out to fulfill their own dreams of their destiny and dropped back in, years later, on the family and life they'd left behind.*

Diya noticed that the photojournalist's ghosts were all steeped in tragedy, malevolent, stereotypically scorned; she wondered what he thought about hers (probably nothing; he seemed not to be truly listening when she spoke, and while this suited her perfectly—that her words could land with no impact—she sensed his gaze growing more searching, more demanding).

But Diya could tell already that he'd made his work the purpose of his life, and that all other commitments and obligations would be, to him, flexible and secondary.

It seemed impossible for him to maintain the level of focus he applied to his work in the rest of his life, especially to quotidian matters. This became evident when she examined the front tire on the scooter he'd lent her and found a hole that looked to be poorly patched, which he'd no doubt forgotten to have fixed properly and then neglected to tell her about. So when the woman in the village handed Diya her cell phone, Diya's first thought was not relief but, *shit*, because she had no relatives, friends, anyone else to call in her (grand)mother's city except the one person she vaguely knew, which was him, and this made her immeasurably sad.

When Diya was six, her mother walked out the door—*Just off to the grocery store for milk*—and never came back. Nothing sinister had happened beyond her mother's own change of heart.

Diya's grandmother had been visiting at the time, as she did a couple times a year. Diya's mother had left a note in the napkin holder in the kitchen, which Diya's grandmother lit on fire over the sink after reading. The note must have given a confession, if not an explanation, enough to result in Diya's grandmother moving in for good to care for her. And then it was just the two of them amid their ghosts: wayward mother/daughter, dead grandfather/husband, never-present, good-for-nothing father / luckily never son-in-law.

The morning after Diya's mother didn't come back, her grandmother simply said: Your mother is gone, but I'm here. That was one of the only times she spoke of it—or would permit them to speak of it—because of course Diya wasn't immune to questions and demands, none of which were acknowledged. She sensed her grandmother felt ashamed, somehow responsible, that she'd caused a misfortune that could never be addressed lest it multiply. Diya walked past whispered phone calls in a language she couldn't speak, caught the shift in her grandmother's weather on certain days—stormy, overcast, prone to rain—and sensed that there was some sporadic but existing line of communication between her mother and grandmother that she would never be privy to, that she couldn't access however much she begged. Her grandmother became a fortress, and particular rooms remained wholly off limits.

Though Diya's mother remained ever-present, taking up permanent residence in the back of her mind, her grandmother quickly absorbed the shock of the physical departure, provided a soft landing in many conspicuous ways. Hers was a terrifying type of devotion: one you could spend your entire life on, twice, even as the person you loved never really came into focus, not within the parameters you'd set. Her grandmother bought a secondhand set of *Good Housekeeping* cookbooks and several pairs of loose-fitting blouses and slacks. She began making mac and cheese, tuna casseroles, and brownies that melted in the mouth, keeping solely to the ingredients and method listed, never deviating to make any dish more palatable in the ways Diya sensed she knew how. They play-acted her grandmother's imagined version of *normalcy*, the childhood and then teenhood her grandmother gathered from TV and movies that Diya's peers were getting. Soccer leagues, piano lessons, Christmas trees and Halloween costumes, barbecues, school dances, and sleepovers, the whole deal. Being abandoned by a parent was difference enough, Diya suspected; her grandmother didn't know or dare to test how much further their local community's tolerance extended.

And yet, in a corner of the pantry, her grandmother kept an altar where Diya would find her in the mornings, palms clasped, summoning her gods. The incense smoke would waft out, leaving apparitions to dissipate in the kitchen. While grabbing her box of cereal, Diya would study the gods' and goddesses' faces, trying to stir a dormant sensation, the legacies embedded within her that had been pulled just out of her grasp. The faces were haughty and unreachable, an expression Diya always imagined her mother wearing, though it wasn't an image from memory.

There were other times, too, that her grandmother's facade dropped, just as it did when she was praying, when an old and deeply rooted superstition would creep into a situation unbidden, the pull to appease the fear of misfortune so strong that her grandmother could not help but command, *sit down and wait, you just sneezed*, or *no no no, don't pass the salt into my hand*. And Diya would walk back from the door she was just about to walk out of, or set the salt back on the table, or throw it over her left shoulder after spilling it, thinking, *here we are still feeding all these ghosts*.

Before Diya walked back to the main road to meet the car the photojournalist was sending for her, she turned around and looked again at the woman's house. I'm leaving now, thank you, she called out, but the woman didn't reappear. The empty water bottle and plate of now-crumbs and phone remained on the porch, and Diya could make out the tread of her own sneakers tracing a path to the house and away from it. She got out her camera and took a picture.

Back at her hotel, she found herself in an overtired state that left her pacing the short distance from her bed to the balcony, pausing every so often to gaze out the open doors onto the glittering buildings below. Around

4:00 a.m. she fell asleep for a short while, fitfully, waking not soon after with the rising sun. On opening her eyes she was still half in the dream she'd been having, coming into wakefulness but trying to dwell in the space her subconscious had constructed.

What her brain had erected was an exact facsimile of the house of the woman who'd helped her. But the dream crept farther than reality had allowed: Diya had entered the home and found a vast courtyard, far larger than the house's exterior suggested. The courtyard was lined by a riot of greenery: short palms; date and banana trees laden with fruit; bougainvillea and jasmine rising up the house's pillars; marigolds, roses, and hibiscus so bright they seemed to imprint on the backs of her eyelids. Beyond the foliage were a number of people that the dream told her were the woman's family members, all of whom were joyful: radiant in the abundance, picking fruits or flowers, reading dog-eared books, eating biscuits on faded blankets, or engaging in spirited conversation with one another. The woman left Diya's side to blend seamlessly into this tableau, back in place with her large, happy, extended family, while Diya edged closer, waiting for a stray smile to be thrown her way, a beckoning hand to wave her over.

That courtyard image remained in her mind all morning: as she called the NGO to explain her absence the day before and was evasive about rescheduling, as she called the photojournalist to thank him for sending the car, as she looked through the photos on her camera, trying to make space on her memory card. The only way to clear the courtyard image of her dreams, she thought, was to replace it, and when she saw again the picture she'd taken the day before outside the woman's house, she was struck by an idea.

She hired a car and set out again for the village. At the woman's house she repeated part of the same routine, the increasingly aggressive knocking, her knuckles smarting, still raw from the day before. The woman finally opened the door, startling to recognize Diya's face, the shock morphing quickly into horror at seeing her there again. Before the woman could ask for an explanation, Diya offered one.

I wanted to thank you for yesterday. I don't know what I would have done if you hadn't helped me. I'm a photographer, and, well, I wanted to bring you this.

She handed over a thin brown paper envelope. The woman looked skeptical but accepted it, peering tentatively inside the top flap though nothing more frightening than a piece of paper could have fit inside. The woman pulled out the single photograph within. As she looked at it, Diya watched the woman cycle through an entire range of emotions—confusion, sadness, anger, awe. Diya knew the woman had seen what she'd intended, what she herself saw in the image: both assistance and aversion, the briefest of bonds between two strangers. And the house behind, bearing witness.

I—don't know what to say, the woman said. It's nothing, what I did. But thank you for this.

More than nothing, Diya said. No one else, if there is anyone else here, opened their door.

There are other people here—, the woman said, cutting herself off. Really, I had what you said in my mind. I thought about your mother, thinking of you, wanting me to help.

Right, Diya said. My mother.

Do you want some biscuits? the woman asked.

Diya agreed. But this time, the woman stood aside from her open front door and motioned for Diya to come inside.

☙

Silence, Diya had learned, could be translated any number of ways. Like a ghost, it was its own presence, large enough to fill a room or small enough to slip through a crack beneath a door. And like a ghost, it was eternally famished, feeding on gaps in Diya's childhood, growing sizeable off words that were swallowed or unsaid, questions never answered.

For instance, questions for a stranger:

What preoccupies you?

    Biscuits

    Footprints

    Salt

Where is your mother?

    Behind a door

    Inside the dream of her own making

    Dancing in the verdant courtyard

What did the woman tell you inside the house?

    The stranger once knocked on every door

      Cajoled, threatened, begged

    No, not the stranger in the mirror

    Worse: the recognizable one

    Yes, of course they opened their doors to her

    Yes, the mother was disguised as a stranger

      She salted the earth in the courtyards

      Nothing could grow, not even in the cribs

    I mean: the misfortune rained down upon them

    I mean: misfortune is a generational flood

      It washes away all evidence of rain

    No, there were never any trees or flowers here

    It's been dirt, just dirt, as long as we've all been alive

I mean: I fear she will return

I mean: I hope she will return

　This time, I'll ask what happened to her

I mean: a ghost can wear anybody's face

When Diya turned eighteen, she told her grandmother where she wanted to go to college and what she wanted to study and build her life's work out of, which was art. Her grandmother's mood immediately shifted, in the familiar way Diya had spent nearly a lifetime tiptoeing around. At that moment, though, on the cusp of starting a different life, or perhaps just the same one in a different setting, Diya's ability to accept her grandmother's reticence collapsed.

Is there some kind of problem? she asked.

No, no problem at all, her grandmother said, with forced cheerfulness. Diya couldn't tell if her grandmother thought she was succeeding in masking her feelings or whether she wanted the dissonance to ring loudly, to stir some sort of guilt in Diya. Either way, it was infuriating.

I'm not stupid, Diya said, I can tell this bothers you.

Still, her grandmother demurred. Diya felt her anger rising and fought to push it down. *She took care of you all these years when no one else would have,* she thought; and yet also, *You never had a father, but you once had a mother and she let that mother leave; she stole that from you; THIEF.*

I'll ask again, Diya said, almost yelling. What exactly is your problem? I'm not doing this anymore, this pretending. Just say what it is you're thinking.

Once she got going, she found she couldn't stop; there were too many grievances that needed to be aired. Her grandmother sat through most of Diya's unprecedented outburst—her railing against the shame they shrouded themselves in, their inability to speak freely about the one topic that consumed both of them—before putting her hand up.

Okay, her grandmother said, wiping tears and composing herself. I understand. How about this: you can ask me one question. Any question. And I promise you I'll answer it honestly.

What her grandmother was offering, then, was not apology but concession. Diya sensed this still cost her grandmother deeply, and that she was not really the person who should be answering any of the myriad questions that had accumulated over the years. So she blurted the freshest one, which was: Why did you go quiet when I said I wanted to make a career out of art?

And her grandmother wrenched an answer out of herself, which was: Because your mother ran off with an artist. She worked as a translator for an author, they became close . . . and that was it, I think. They wanted their work, themselves, together, that's all, and that was it.

Later, when Diya graduated art school, she invited her grandmother to the closing day of the seniors' exhibition. Her grandmother stopped before an image of a hilly green landscape devoid of people, the colors rendered soft and malleable so that the photograph gave the impression of a painting.

Is this yours? she asked. It's beautiful.

It was not; her images hung in the adjoining room. Diya had spent the year on a series of digital collages that inserted figures from her family photographs into scenes from vintage postcards from her (grand)mother's city. She hadn't mentioned the project to her grandmother, worried about her response.

It's mine, she said, losing her will, wanting instead to bask in the celebratory mood, which was so much easier. She steered her grandmother out of the exhibition and toward the spread of canapés outside.

So the single answer she'd gotten earlier was the last time they spoke of her mother. Diya had moved away after school and flitted from job to job for years, periodically dropping in on her grandmother, who had then died, unexpectedly. That detail about her mother had to be enough for Diya, or at least she told herself it was. It made sense that her mother had been a translator. That was what Diya had been grieving already, all along: the loss of her mother as an intermediary, a medium through which to communicate with the ancestors she had no names for.

The morning after her second trip to the village, Diya woke again with a dream of the place fading, her hands balled into fists and her sheets sweat soaked. I have to let this go, she thought to herself, even as she dialed the front desk for another car, even as she traveled the now-familiar road back to the village. The woman seemed less surprised to see Diya this time. She opened the door on the tenth knock or so, before Diya had to resort to pounding.

Hello, Aunty, Diya said. The woman had introduced herself as Amrita, but Diya couldn't bring herself to use a first name on a woman of her age.

You again, Amrita said, but there was a hint of a smile on her face. More photographs?

I didn't bring anything this time, sorry. I just couldn't stop thinking about this place.

Strange, Amrita said. Most try not to think about this place at all. For good reason.

Why— Diya began, but Amrita interrupted.

No more biscuits, I'm afraid, but I just made some bajjis, if you want some.

She left the door ajar, and the wind slammed it shut suddenly with a loud bang, startling them both. Amrita looked over nervously at the neighboring house. Diya followed her gaze and noticed two heads quickly ducking back into the doorway, trying in vain not to be seen.

So there are other people here, Diya said. Do you want to invite them to join us?

They won't come, Amrita said. She looked again at the neighbor's house and back at Diya. But I can ask.

She walked over and was gone for some time. Diya drew semicircles with the toe of her sneaker in the dust. When Amrita came back, she was followed by a crowd, mostly men and women of similar ages, white-haired, with no children or younger adults in sight.

There were others who'd seen you here, Amrita said. They wanted to know who you were. I told them about the photograph you gave me. I wanted to show them.

Inside her house, Amrita had propped the photo up on a teak chair in the courtyard. It sat there like one of the house's inhabitants: the house itself, or its exterior; how it appeared to others.

Diya stood a short distance away with Amrita while the crowd took turns examining the photograph. After, a man in a stiff button-down and dress pants approached her.

I don't have any photographs of my house, not like this, he said. It's been in my family for generations. Do you think you could photograph my house too?

Diya agreed, and other residents approached her to make similar requests. She rented a scooter and found herself going back and forth on that same city-to-village stretch many times over the next several months, drinking

Limca or tea or water on the neighbor's porches, eating an assortment of snacks offered to her, and periodically remembering her camera, raising it only when the moment felt right, which resulted not from her knowledge of proper lighting or ideal composition but a nudge somewhere below her ribs that told her *now, now, NOW.*

After a time, some residents began asking for portraits of themselves, which Diya took too, coming back each time laden with prints, the once-identical houses becoming irrevocably distinct because of the people she now knew to live within each of them.

For instance:

	Visit 1	Visit 2	Visit 3	Visit 4	Visit 5
House 102	x	x	x	widower one daughter, two sons whiskey, neat	[she has her face] [never just one]
House 223	x	x	arranged marriage no children husband former pilot wife homemaker	[an easy companionship, if lacking in passion] [but they were wished for, dearly] [never more at home than in the clouds] [can I be more than someone's grounding?]	[yes, it's lacking] [by her: moreso] [still prays during turbulence] [feigns prayer while looking up: god, that endless sky]
House 316	x	x	x	eye doctor, now nearly blind due to cataracts plays piano by touch	[having experienced both, prefers the blur] [& weeps: what other clarity?]

On one visit, when Diya wrapped up her day at Amrita's, she finally decided to ask.

Oh yes, the writing above the doorways, Amrita said. It means "come tomorrow," you see, to ward off the stranger.

Over these weeks, Diya's meetings with the photojournalist over drinks at their respective hotel bars multiplied. She told herself it was casual and easy, two foreigners seeing each other solely because they shared a country of residence in common and no deeper connection. But she felt them slipping into some other precarious liminal space in which he might ask something of her directly.

Once, a person:

(a) *left his phone on the bar, face up while he went to the bathroom. The lock screen lit up with an incoming call, a number associated with a picture, an apparition that materialized of a woman holding a toddler, both cheesing for the camera.*

(b) *removed a piece of jewelry from his left ring finger, leaving a spectral, untanned area that was as noticeable as what was usually present there.*

(c) *looked away from the ringing phone, feeling like she was invading his privacy, and when he returned from the bathroom she didn't ask him about it, not then, not after, even as it sat in the air between them.*

One evening the photojournalist told her to meet him at his room, he wanted to give her a galley of his forthcoming book of photographs. When she walked in, she noticed a spread of food laid out in his sitting area.

I ordered us dinner, he said. I thought we could just hang out up here.

She spotted charred kebabs and rich curries amid steaming cartons of rice. He'd clearly forgotten she was vegetarian. She made herself a plate that was largely liquids; if he noticed her picking around the meat, he didn't say.

As she finished she noticed him staring at her, and he moved to sit next to her on the loveseat she'd claimed. He reached out and thumbed the strap of her dress, tucked an escaped tendril from her braid behind her ear. She was unable to shake the feeling that he was handling her like a camera—practiced and attuned to precision, but manipulating her more like a machine than a warm body. She, too, a challenge to unlock, like how the right amount of fiddling and preparation could yield the most poignant photograph of a ruined landscape.

He took her hand and stood up. What kind of person am I, she thought, as she stood up, too, and felt his other hand on the small of her back. A secret / a stranger / a closed book—

But that wasn't really the right question, she knew. It was: What kind of person did she want to be?

I have to leave, she said, and did.

❦

The exhibition, called *Trust*, opened five months after Diya first set foot in the village. When all the photographs had been taken, Diya had laid them on the floor of her hotel room and seen the thread running through, clear as if she'd known it beforehand. The subtle shift in gaze in the portraits, downward-cast to straight-on, the body language softening, the progression from the paths to the porches to, eventually, the courtyard inside. The residents' one condition to granting consent for the exhibition was that they write the catalogue's introduction:

> *We, who've lived here for generations in these houses, wish to craft a living archive for ourselves of the facades we've erected, the ones we've lived behind, the protective measures we have deployed against misfortune, which dwells in and among these buildings as much as joy, sorrow, pleasure, pain, remain sibling ghosts. That this haunted architecture may be seen if only to convey the message that not everyone you don't know is a stranger and not every stranger is someone you don't know. For we, as all of us may be if we are honest, are intimately familiar with our own ghosts, awake between the lines of the stories we could tell in our sleep.*

Diya invited everyone from the village to the opening, offering to arrange transport. Though none of the residents expressly declined, she knew already from the way they shook their heads or said *maybe* that they wouldn't come. At Amrita's request, she also invited her daughter who lived in the city, who said she would.

The night of the opening, Diya wore the same dress she'd worn that night in the photojournalist's room. He'd left the city—drawn off on an extended assignment in another state, which he'd relayed to her in a curt text. Part of her wished he'd been able to come, wanted him to see this exact part of her, wanted to talk shop with him about what she'd created. Part of her was grateful he hadn't, that she could leave him on her life's periphery. Just a memory to surface unexpectedly: when she saw his name, saw his dimples on another face, ate sad food off a paper plate in a hotel room.

Midway through the night a woman walked into the gallery alone. She was perhaps a generation older than Diya, smartly dressed, her demeanor self-assured. Her face looked strikingly similar to Diya's own, like someone who could play Diya's mother in a movie. The woman made a loop around the gallery, pausing at each photograph to look carefully at what was depicted, a twinkle of recognition in her eyes. When the woman reached *The Helping Hand, 2022, gelatin silver print on paper,* Diya joined her.

Your mother, right? She really saved me that day.

Yeah, the woman said, she told me about it after. I couldn't believe she opened the door. Really, that any of them agreed to do this.

It took time, Diya said. But of course you'd know that.

The woman gestured at the gallery, eyes wide. Anyway, look at all this. Your own mother must be so proud of you.

Well— Diya said. Yes.

The woman nodded, smiled.

Actually, Diya said, no. Or really, I wouldn't know. I haven't seen her in decades. But what I really want to ask is, what was it like for you there?

Oh, the woman said. Her face had dropped at Diya's revelation, but she allowed the conversation to shift. Let me tell you.

Amrita's daughter spoke transparently of her yearning, above all else, to leave that place, how it had felt calcified in fear and shame, that she worried for her mother but didn't visit enough, had trouble bringing herself to go back. She'd been in the city since her college years, studying to become an actuary and now spending her days immersed in statistics about death, quantifying risk and harm in actual, tangible ways. She had her own family there, daughters, a partner, an apartment with nosy neighbors who took every opportunity to drop by unannounced.

Diya sensed Amrita's daughter had at last found the right listener, someone with a degree of context. She let the unbroken stream continue uninterrupted, ignoring the other attendees who tried to pull her attention away. When Amrita's daughter finished, she told Diya she had to run but hoped to see her again. Diya watched her leave, returned the genuine smile and wave she received as Amrita's daughter turned back at the door. As if it really were that simple: to fill silence with a stranger, to finally say all the unsaid things out loud.

Empires Have Been Destroyed

I.

If the right street in Bandra had been whispered to you, it is said, a street named after a canonized Catholic whose very name you could hold in your mouth like a prayer to a patron saint, you could take a rickshaw to the area and have it drop you a safe distance away, perhaps outside one of the civil servants' squat two-story bungalows, because people who lived in those houses had no need to go wandering the quarter on foot after work, pretending not to be lost and refusing to ask for directions, having instead the luxury of the right connections and moreover the benefit of Gothic-crowned windows and porched second-story balconies on which they could safely imbibe.

It would take some effort to find the correct non-descript apartment building, though after the day you'd had, you might not mind the searching. Eventually you'd come across a pav bhaji or boiled eggs vendor, parked in an unassuming residential side street, who'd recognize that particular questing look about you. And he'd nod and incline his head toward one of the street-facing windows, expecting, correctly, that you'd stop at his cart on your way out of that building in return for this unspoken guidance.

Up three flights of stairs you'd finally find Ana's place, though when she opened the door a crack to answer you'd call her *aunty*. The apartment would be even smaller than you imagined on seeing it from the outside, only the one window for the living room and in the unseen inner depths probably a kitchen and one narrow bedroom. Someone—for the living room would be full already, as if you were late to a gathering in progress—would pull you up a plastic chair, or a stool, or a crate to sit on, and you would perch by the dingy floral-patterned curtains pulled shut and join their conversation, groups of mostly men but also a few women, college students or intellectuals or jobless down-on-their-lucks or shopkeepers or accountants. Depending on the crowd, you'd debate the virtues of politicians like Nehru versus Bose, or directors like Satyajit Ray and his realist films versus Mehboob Khan and his fateful pairing of actors Raj Kapoor and Nargis. Or, when Ana brought you the glass of what you'd asked for, neat—snake juice or white lightning or, if you ditch the euphemisms, just plain toddy or moonshine or feni— you'd talk to her instead, ask her how business had been of late, get some advice for your troubles or maybe even a suggestion about a girl of marriageable age from a good family you should meet. If it was extra busy, her daughter Mari would also be flitting around, carrying trays of drinks for patrons, but under Ana's watchful eye any conversations with Mari could be only cursory, a few snippets tossed in passing.

Six years into prohibition, this situation could be expected, even this division of labor: mother, often widowed, brews and tends bar; adult daughter, often longing for a different life, reluctantly helps out. The tide of independence, while washing out foreign rule, had pulled in with it a temperance movement that deemed liquor a serious defect. In certain communities, where perhaps this view was not as deep-seated, where perhaps one's relatives had been toddy-tappers or where one's family had been guarding a special kaju feni recipe for hundreds of years, this situation could also be viewed as an opportunity. Even before the enactment of the law in '49, those in the building already knew Ana brewed the best feni in the neighborhood, stopping by more often than she would have liked for a sip from her storeroom cache. When her husband died a few years after the law's passage, killed in a road accident, Ana had few options to feed herself and her daughter other than to capitalize on her existing renown.

Some said her husband drank too much, that so many years as a seafaring merchant had made him wary of land, eager to replicate the sensation of the ground always shifting beneath his feet. That this was why the lorry he was driving had veered off a well-lit road into a ditch marked by a sprawling banyan tree. If you became a regular patron, you knew never to mention the man to Ana or Mari, never to question the decisions they'd made to provide for themselves. After all, you yourself would be sitting on a stool in an unknown woman's apartment, beneath a wooden cross from an unfamiliar faith, peering at unfamiliar faces in the dim lighting of thick curtains paired with sparsely placed lamps, knowing nevertheless that dark was falling outside, and soon you'd have to leave and go back to your own home, undoubtedly somewhere distant. When you left, you'd stop first for pav bhaji from the vendor outside to whom you'd implicitly promised your business, and the whole journey home you'd hope the smell of raw onions would mask not only the reek of alcohol but also any little lies you'd have to tell—to your spouse, your partner, the rickshaw driver, a run-into acquaintance, a policeman, or a passing stranger—about where you'd just come from, a place that was not supposed to exist.

II.

If you asked a neighbor when Ana had moved into her place, it would seem to them that she had always been there. But really it had only been a couple of decades, from the time just after she'd gotten married in a little church in Candolim, wearing a long, lacy white dress and with her skinny arms lined with the colorful glass bangles she'd later have to break over her husband's coffin. The day following her wedding, she'd worn the customary red sari and set off with her husband for Bombay. Though her husband had grown up in the next town over from her, he'd been living in Bombay for a year and already kept a rented flat there, which was ostensibly now for the two of them though really mostly for her. They lived in Bombay for its proximity to the port, where Ana would see her husband off every few weeks for another of his postings at sea.

Their leaving was the first time Ana had been outside Candolim, and when she arrived in the city, with its trams and noise and lack of swaying palms and sheer *density*, it seemed an impossible place. But she took comfort in the enclave of Bandra, which faced the same waters she'd grown up with—the Arabian Sea—and where so many fellow Goans lived it was possible to close one's eyes and hear the waves and the Konkani and imagine one's self back, for a moment, in a formative place.

Though her husband was rarely home those initial few years, Ana managed, eventually, to get pregnant, though just the once, which she told herself and her family was more than enough. With the help of a few community midwives, while her husband was rounding Cape Comorin en route to Sri Lanka, Ana delivered a healthy baby girl she named Mari, because that name was a variant of Mary/Maria that was said to mean *beloved*.

The neighbors who saw Ana and Mari out together—and it was usually just the two of them, from the beginning—thought the name was fitting, for the girl was undoubtedly loved. Ana pushed her daughter around the quarter in a black pram given to her by a neighbor whose children were now all school aged. She was often observed stopping to jiggle the metal push-handle, urging the sticky wheels to resume their track. The girl never protested during these walks, not a cry or a peep, and later, when she grew old enough to explore the neighborhood on her own two feet, she remained thoughtful and quiet, keeping hold of her mother's hand while they made the same afternoon circuit around the shaded, leafy streets. As the neighbors watched her age, it became obvious that Mari would become the spitting image of her mother—short with thick curly hair and a round, open face that seemed to invite the spilling of confidences.

Though neighbors often commented that the girl was too introverted, Ana brushed off the matter of Mari's childhood silence, knowing it actually masked a whirring brain that was constantly cataloguing and questioning its observations. During the long days alone in the apartment, Ana would struggle to find ways to entertain her daughter, new activities to replace the ones Mari had already mastered and tired of. The daily walks persisted because Mari approached them like a spot-the-difference game: amid the usual paths and routines, she would look for what was out of the ordinary—a tree that had begun to flower, a stray dog with a new back paw limp, a colorful rangoli freshly painted outside the gates of one of the bungalows.

It is said that this is how the feni brewing began: a difference, born out of Ana's desire to occupy the slow-passing hours, as much for Mari as for herself. After Mari began going to school, dressed in her pressed blue pinafore uniform and carefully pinned-up plaits, walking anticlimactically out the door following the morning's getting-ready whirlwind, Ana found wading through the sluggish middle of the day suddenly untenable, shaped as it had previously been entirely around the girl's presence. One day Mari came home from school and the kitchen floor was covered by a plastic tarp. Laid on top was a layer of flat rocks, on top of which was a pile of what appeared to be small, plump red peppers. This was Mari's first introduction to cashew apples, which the two of them then proceeded to crush underfoot gleefully, Mari letting go for once of her meticulousness, and Ana relishing the squelching between her toes, a feeling she had never forgotten but hadn't dared hope to replicate.

Fermenting was achieved through a complicated setup of pipes and copper pots in the storeroom off the kitchen. Ana tinkered with the mechanics for months before perfecting its timing and arrangement. The contraption was not built for scale, so later it was useful that Ana had built up years of bottles (despite what she'd thought was an unfailing generosity of pouring with her neighbors) before she ever had a need to sell the liquor. Ana thought it lucky that the storeroom had a tiny window overlooking the gully behind the apartment building, for she worried a bit about harboring heady vapors in the kitchen and the apartment. No one who didn't live in the building ventured into the gully, and even so, the faint sweet-and-slightly-sickly aroma that could sometimes be caught back there was untraceable to any specific one of the array of tiny windows, all of which the building's residents kept open for ventilation and cross breeze.

The neighbors liked to note, among themselves and sometimes to Ana, that Mari grew up like the feni-making process, in three stages. The first press produced a mild alcohol called arrack, the second, cazulo, a bit stronger, and the third and final press resulted in feni, which, with its nearly 50 percent alcohol volume, was liable to knock you out. Mari's meekness in childhood gave way to a slight edge once she started school, one that might catch you if you said something stupid or that could be interpreted as insulting. By the time she reached adulthood—by which time her father had come back from the sea ill-adjusted to land, and soon after made her mother a widow who ran a clandestine bar out of their living room—she was noticeably hardened. Some said she sharpened herself as a means of protecting Ana, that this was a role she felt duty-bound now to play. But what didn't change about Mari was that she revealed her true self only to her mother; she dreamt of moving out of the city, away from the dreaded sea, inland to a small, quiet place where she could be a grade-school teacher, maybe or maybe not getting married. She said she would do all this if there were enough money to do so, which she knew there wouldn't be. So the other conditions precedent to the dream thankfully didn't have to be mentioned: that Mari was reluctant to do any of this unless her mother was no longer living, and that Ana wanted her daughter to be able to control, as far as possible, the course of her own life, but this required Mari to first stay close and cultivate a potent mixture of desire, pragmatism, and skill.

III.

If you frequented Ana's place, you'd understand quickly that she brewed more than just kaju feni; she could craft liquor from nearly any fruit or vegetable, fresh or gone a bit rotten, from its flesh, its pith, its peels. The same alcoholic bite remained, but the taste might be laced with the slightest hint of tomatoes or coconut or beets or jackfruit or carrots or papaya, or whatever caught her eye at the market. She perused roadside stalls like a magpie, alighting without fail on whichever fruits a seller had taken the time beforehand to polish to a bright sheen. Her experimentation would reach its peak around the Christmas holidays, when you could often find mulled wine on offer, crafted not from grapes but perhaps from pineapple, and spiced with ginger and cloves and cinnamon, and served with fried flower-shaped kalkals, leaving the mouth feeling festive enough to match the more-jovial-than-usual atmosphere in the cramped living room.

It is said Ana's cache dwindled faster than she imagined, that she hadn't envisioned prohibition lasting as long

as it did. She'd thought a country so accustomed to spirits would soon come to its senses, realizing the detriment
of driving business to a black market. The neighbors and
patrons chatted often of raids they'd heard about, men
climbing out of windows and students fleeing through
back gullies, policemen kicking down doors only to find
their colleagues calmly sipping drinks inside, aunties who
showed up at jails as pretend relatives to bail out their own
patrons. Ana was keenly aware of the danger; this was
well-known. As any given night wore on, she'd start to
wring her hands, shushing any increase in volume, wanting nothing more than to kick everyone out of her house
though the patrons, understanding their position as guests
in someone's home, remained unfailingly well-mannered.
Mari took advantage of the fact that she was readily welcomed into any ongoing conversation due to her status as
Ana's daughter; she quietly memorized all the overheard
troubles and secrets, filing them away for future leverage
in case anyone had a change of heart, a sudden urge to
report the goings-on to the police.

Once a week Ana and Mari would count the remaining bottles and plan what they'd produce the following
week. Ana was amazed that one law and a few strokes
of a pen had caused demand to suddenly reach a height
that would continue, no matter her output, to outmatch
her possible supply. It was inevitable that there came an

accounting in which the bottles—which had once been stored all over the apartment, in closets and cabinets and under the bed—numbered only five, enough for only a few nights more of patrons, perhaps more if she diluted the liquor or served it only with soda, hoping no one would notice save for remarking on a less vicious hangover the day after.

On becoming a patron of Ana's, you also became privy to a whole new stream of gossip, like stumbling upon a moss-hidden cave that sheathed a long, snaking underground river. You'd hear about all the illicit stills in the city, all the living room bars, all the means by which liquor was spirited in and around the city: false-bottom milk cans, bicycle tires, hot-water bottles, manholes covering barrels of fermenting mash, hiding spots in presumed-to-be-haunted swamps, lepers whom the police were loath to search and whom it was said could not be fingerprinted anyway. This was the vast and secret system that Ana and Mari were certainly conscious of but refused to consider themselves a part of, at least until the day the liquor almost ran out.

It is said that it was Mari who first suggested the plan, who volunteered herself to procure some mash they might quick ferment with ammonium chloride, which she'd heard some aunties were using to speed up the process. The mash would be cheap enough, maybe five rupees a gallon for the type of slop a pig might eat, potato peels and molasses waste and mostly brown or rotten fruits. If they rearranged the shelves in the kitchen a bit, gave away some clothes and moved some steel vessels to the bedroom almirahs, the space could easily accommodate a few extra drums for fermentation. And it was Mari who would need to go, because her plan was to conceal the several-gallon jug of mash beneath a loose and flowing top, so that any person or policeman she might pass would assume her an innocent pregnant woman.

The solution was sound, but it took a few days, as you might understand, to convince Ana of it. She worried about embroiling her daughter further in these activities, to take what she'd circumscribed to the safe space of the home—a respectful and genteel gathering it was easy enough to pretend was a dinner party of friends—out into the world, that vast, seedy network of secretive and deceptive dealings. But the rent came due, the groceries needed buying, the gas for the stove needed replacing. Eventually Ana agreed to send Mari for the mash, but only if she'd take a patron with her, one of Mari's choice, someone who could serve as a male chaperone but moreover as a bodyguard of sorts.

Mari was friendly with many of the patrons but not friends with any of them in particular, given that she kept everyone but Ana at a polite but cold distance. She didn't choose any of the many men who were obviously sweet on her or any of the ones who ignored her completely. It is said she settled on Dinesh, a watchman from a neighboring building, because of his occupation, and because of his lean but muscular form; he seemed like someone who might be able to protect her if the need arose, or at least to have an elevated eye and ear for danger. He agreed even before Ana offered him a few rupees for his trouble, which Mari thought boded well for their mission.

In the bottom of their almirah, Ana found an old beige cotton salwar kameez she'd meant to give away long ago, one she'd worn when she was pregnant during the summer months with Mari and could barely stand the touch of fabric on her skin. From an already-torn silk sari Ana ripped several strands and braided them together into two ropes that would not chafe against her daughter's skin. She used these to tie a large earthenware jug around Mari's belly, high, as if she were carrying a girl, so that any nosy aunties who saw her would cluck in pity and leave her alone. The effect must have been powerful when they both looked at Mari in the mirror, her cheeks flushed and her posture extra straight in compensation for the new weight. Neighbors who knew Ana imagined she must have brushed away a tear before Mari could see it, for that would have revealed the wish Ana hadn't even known she'd made until she saw this vision of her proud and pregnant daughter.

Mari knew from the neighborhood gossip that Dinesh had kept his job for so many years because he was prompt, without fail, where others in similar local positions frequently arrived hours late or not at all. At noon exactly, as arranged, Dinesh knocked at Ana's door, and he, too, was struck by the glowing and determined girl who answered. Let's go, Mari said to Dinesh, already walking past him into the hallway. We have a long way to go and not much time.

IV.

If you regularly stopped by Ana's or even another aunty's place, you'd likely have guessed where Mari was headed for the mash, some morass of a hiding place, the nearest lowland. And, indeed, Mari and Dinesh took a rickshaw across the city-island close to where it came to its end like an open crab claw, past the Mithi River and down to the mudflats near Sewri Fort, around where the flocks of flamingos would congregate if it were winter, standing unmoving in the shallow marsh, their washed-out pink making them look like marble statues abandoned to the swamp tides. There Mari and Dinesh left their chappals on a stretch of dry sand and rolled up their pant and salwar legs, wading ankle- to knee-deep and searching the thicket of mangroves until they found a root tied with a half-submerged yellow ribbon. They waited by the root until eventually a man—really, a boy—who had been loitering in the area came splashing over, understanding why they'd come. Mari gave the boy the money he demanded, more than she'd hoped but less than she'd expected. The boy pointed to another root nearby, where they now noticed a rope that extended beneath the surface and which, Dinesh and the boy straining together, eventually pulled up a drum of mash that freed itself from the swamp's hold with a sickening sucking sound.

The boy left them, then, to fill on their own the jug Mari had brought, and it is said that this is when the incident happened—after the boy returned to his post on the dry sand and Mari moved deeper into the root tunnel to pull up the edge of her top so she could undo the ropes holding the jug in place. Ana had thought, of course, about making the knots extra secure, but she'd forgotten about making them easy to untie. Mari struggled to reach a fat knot sitting against her sacrum, where her arms could barely bend back around to manipulate the rope, and eventually she called Dinesh over to help. But: his fingers lingered too long in the undoing, stroked the sides of her bare waist as he worked, resisted releasing her for a long moment as she pushed away from him, turning to hand him the empty jug. She looked at him with disgust and betrayal in her eyes, which Dinesh did not acknowledge. Instead, he arranged his face to look indignant, as if what she'd felt was accidental, incidental, enough to make Mari wonder if she'd imagined what had happened, but not enough to doubt her own instincts, honed from years in crowded buses and trams and packed stations and sadly not having to imagine.

When the jug was filled, Mari retied the knots herself, facing them now forward, and the two returned to Ana's, Mari leaving as much space between her and Dinesh as was possible in the rickshaw and keeping her gaze fixed ahead but unfocused at some point in the distance. They arrived just after five in the evening, when the living room was already near-full with patrons. Dinesh melted into the crowd and Mari retreated to the bedroom, telling her mother she was tired from the journey and wanted to lie down. Days passed and the fresh mash fermented in the kitchen's new drums. By the following weekend the crowd had peaked again, and it included Dinesh, who posted himself in a prime position in the corner by the windows, from where one could observe the entire room.

Ana enlisted Mari to help serve everyone, hoping her new concoction would be to the patrons' tastes. She and Mari drank nearly none of what they brewed themselves, except on holidays or special occasions. At one point Ana could not resist peeking into the living room from her post in the kitchen, wanting to watch the reactions to the latest batch of liquor. What she saw, instead, was the wide berth Mari was keeping around Dinesh, how she left his drinks on the table next to him rather than let him take them from the tray in her hands, how she made no acknowledgement of any words he spoke to her, refusing even to make eye contact. Later, she confronted her daughter about this behavior, knowing something was amiss, and in Mari's hesitance to reveal what had happened, her reluctance to explain, she understood immediately what Dinesh had done and was overcome with the desire to kill him. But she settled for promising Mari that Dinesh would no longer be welcome at their place, and the next time he arrived he would be told so and removed forcibly if necessary.

Weeks passed, though, and Dinesh did not return. Ana felt this was a bit of luck, as she was slightly concerned that he might react violently to a confrontation and notification of his permanent barring. But a month later he did show up, and there was not even time for Ana to raise the issue she wanted to because he barged into the full living room screaming and cursing until a few of the upstairs neighbors came down to see what was happening.

That *witch* Ana poisoned me, he yelled, refusing to move farther than the doorway, where he had the attention of everyone in the room as well as the outside hallway. I nearly died! She'll pay for this, I'm calling the police here, you'll see.

A group of students who were all fond of Mari saw her face go pale as she watched this scene; it is said that seeing this spurred them to action. Refraining from loud and boorish behavior at Ana's was an unspoken rule, because doing so obviously drew attention to the gathering and put everyone in the apartment at risk. The students grabbed Dinesh's elbows and dragged him down the stairs to the street, where they quieted him and sent him away. Ana's apartment, meanwhile— after the threat of possible police involvement—had mostly cleared itself by the time the students came back upstairs.

They told Ana and Mari what they had been able to piece together from Dinesh's incoherent ramblings: he had apparently fallen deathly ill after his last visit to Ana's, had been bedridden with crippling stomach pains that had only just dissipated. Someone had apparently once told Dinesh of an exorcist near Candolim, and he had connected this in his mind with Ana, believing her capable of witchcraft or some devious treachery that enabled her to poison him deliberately. He hadn't proposed any motive for Ana's alleged poisoning, though, which the group (some of whom were law students) said they found suspicious. This is how what Dinesh had done to Mari came to be known—in the silence following the students' summary, as Ana was looking at her daughter questioningly, wondering if she should reveal what the two of them knew of Dinesh's character, Mari simply burst out with it.

No one was sure whether it was the witch rumor or the impending police visit that was keeping patrons away, but in any event the next few days at Ana's were slow ones and the living room remained an empty sitting place, never transforming upon a coded knock on the door into a lively neighborhood pub. The neighbors speculated about Ana, wondering whether she did possess an interest in the occult, whether there was something more to all the ingredients she kept lying around, all the brewing she did in her kitchen. Some said they'd once seen the cross on the wall of Ana's living room hanging upside down, that the clocks in there were all stopped, that there were witches who could eat an entire apple without touching the skin, who knew all the ways to kill a man without leaving a mark. Some said, more quietly, that regardless of whether or not Ana had done it, Dinesh had deserved that poisoning.

The quiet ended on a Monday evening, close to the witching hour, when the police presumed the inhabitants of the building would be sleeping and thus unprepared.

They kicked in Ana's door, which brought her and Mari out of the bedroom immediately, dressed in long nightgowns and rubbing their eyes against the three flashlight beams aimed at their faces.

Go ahead, search, Ana told them, and she and Mari returned to the bedroom where they perched on their beds, listening to the men's crashing and trampling progress through the apartment. The policemen opened every cabinet, checked within, below, and behind each item of furniture, and rapped on every inch of wall and floor to see if there were false panels located anywhere. In the kitchen they found only a few copper pots for washing, and some root vegetables piled in the storeroom. One of the men held a knife over Ana and Mari's thin mattresses, about to begin ripping them open, when the constable stopped him.

There's nothing here, the constable said. Pick up that mattress, do you think anything of note to us can possibly be hidden in there?

The officer let the mattress drop to the floor, looking chastened.

Sorry for disturbing you, madam, the constable added, to Ana. We'll be on our way now.

Ana saw the policemen to the door, shutting it firmly and quickly behind them. As she had not acknowledged the crowd of neighbors that had gathered in the hallway, eager to learn the latest news, they murmured for several minutes about how this reticence was out of character.

V.

If you knew Ana solely from her place, you probably would not have been invited to her funeral. But you might have heard that it was held in the same little church in Candolim where she'd gotten married, that it was surprisingly well attended, with quite a few strange faces milling about whom none of the relatives recognized, men in ill-fitting dark suits they wore like uniforms so they could not be distinguished or recognized, who came with well-wishes but left before their relationship to Ana could be probed any further. Mari, of course, would have been there, on leave from her job at an English medium school in Pune. She'd come to Candolim near the end to care for her mother, who herself had returned to the place of her birth when she'd felt the first twinges of her ripe old age, an unfortunately incurable ailment.

And if you knew Ana from her place because you were the one who had smashed into it and searched it one night many years earlier, you certainly would not have been invited to her funeral. But being a well-connected local commissioner now, you would have heard through the grapevine of its occurrence. Ana's name had dogged you for a few years after the search, some believing it impossible you'd found nothing incriminating at her place, that either you or your colleagues must have yourselves been patrons willing to turn a blind eye, or else been bewitched or charmed against your will to do so.

In light of that, you'd never told anyone about the bottle that had been delivered to you at the police station a few weeks after the search, placed on your desk by someone during a lunch hour when the place was empty and it was possible to slip in and out unnoticed. It was the best kaju feni you'd ever tasted, so good you could not bear to drink it all, having no hope of procuring anything as perfect ever again. You'd been glad, in fact, that you'd saved it, because this allowed you to pour yourself a glass and toast its presumed maker on the day you heard of Ana's death.

Until the funeral—and despite the previous brief wave of suspicion—no one had mentioned her name to you in a very long time. Not since prohibition had been lifted in the '60s, too late to stop or control the large and sprawling underworld that had taken over the business of bootlegging and adapted that underground network for a range of increasingly violent criminal activities. In light of the arrests you'd made in the past few decades, you could almost laugh at your near-bust of a young widow and her daughter. They'd showed no fear whatsoever when you and your team had barged in. You'd been thinking of this when you opened every cabinet yourself and found nothing, when you bid them farewell, when you went downstairs to find the rest of your men eating hot pav bhaji from the vendor parked outside. Even and especially when you'd gone back to their place after receiving the bottle and found no sign of Ana or Mari there. All you'd seen was the movement of curtains in neighboring apartments as you walked away down the street, the briefest flash of faces you knew had just been pressed against the windows there.

A Working Theory of Optical Illusions

I learned today that my mother's room had a view. The hospital complex was so labyrinthine I'd assumed her window looked out on a blank wall or some kind of building innards, copper pipes and errant wiring. Instead, the blinds collapsed to reveal the full moon, low as if it had been pinned there for the room's inhabitant to admire. The distant hills were caught up in the beam and I spied, for a moment, the glittering spike of a radio tower. In all these weeks it had never occurred to me to pull up the blinds or even tilt the slats. I wasn't sure if my mother had requested the insularity, wishing to cocoon herself, or if the blinds were opened only during the hours when I was not there. While I looked out the window, the night nurse stood by the doorless bathroom, studying her callused hands. It was she who had suggested we open the window. When someone dies, she whispered, it's good to give the soul a place to go.

My mother's death was not shocking to me; she had been ailing for months, so much so that I began to hope I would not have to watch her reach the bottom of her seemingly endless deterioration. The only surprise at the end was what she said to me. We had been looking at one of my baby scrapbooks, gingerly turning pages already half-unbound from years of handling. On the third page, we arrived at our only complete family photo: my mother, head thrown back, laughing; me, cradled in my mother's arms, napping; my father, arms crossed, smiling. In my childhood, the longer his absence continued, the more I returned to this picture, sleuthing for clues, attempting to dismantle the growing mythos around his character. Did his crossed arms foretell a closed-off personality? Did his slight lean toward my mother indicate remorse about his coming abandonment? There were any number of traits to read into the picture, any number of ways to will an absence into a presence. When I grew old enough, I learned to read into my mother's silences instead.

I hadn't seen the photograph in quite some time when my mother stopped at its page. She took my hand, squeezing it gently, as she always did when I pulled a chair over to her bedside. For so many years it had been just the two of us; I'd grown used to this kind of easy intimacy.

Lately, honey, she said, I've had quite a bit of time to think. I know you value certainty, hard-won truths.

Here she paused and then peeled the family photograph off the page. I stared at her, wondering if she was relishing this moment, knowing her to be passionate, prone to drama. She had also developed an otherworldly sort of clarity in the later stages of her illness that I found unsettling. After a brief glance at me, my mother ripped the photograph in half. I neither gasped nor moved to stop her. I thought it best to let the scene unfold as she had planned it.

The man in the photograph, she continued, was a work acquaintance who had come by our apartment just after I was born, who had happened to pose that day for a picture in the dim living room. She'd gravitated to this colleague because he was a fellow immigrant from India, the sole other one in the export-import company in Jackson Heights where my mother worked as a secretary. Their relationship, though, had only ever been a friendship, which ended when he returned, shortly after my birth, to Hyderabad.

I imagine most daughters say this about their mothers, but mine was truly a beautiful woman. Primarily in ways a photograph could rarely capture: twinkling eyes, hair to midback swinging like a black sheet in the breeze, sharp features shifting, constantly, into expressions of delight or gleeful mischief. We were often mistaken in public for sisters. I was well aware that in her early twenties, my mother had been plucked from the cement steps outside her college in Mumbai to debut in the first film by an up-and-coming director. After that my mother decided to finish her degree in the United States and never returned to India. The director went on to direct only one more film—a stratospheric success—following which he retreated entirely from public life and had not been seen or heard from since. This man, according to my mother, was my biological father.

The initial shock dissipated within a few minutes. Clearheaded once more, I found my emotions intact where I'd left them, no force of betrayal altering their trajectories. Having been raised in a communal culture, my mother knew there was no more valuable currency than a secret kept to and for yourself, away from the prying eyes and ears of acquaintances and relatives. I learned early on that details were to be carefully curated and life lived on a need-to-know basis. Sharing started with the self and emanated outward in concentric circles, to each other, to extended family, to friends, to strangers, and so on, in decreasing order of transparency. In light of this, however hurt I might have felt by my mother's revelation about my father's identity, I respected her determination that for all the previous years of my life I had not needed to know it.

After some time the night nurse cleared her throat, which I understood as a gentle nudge to leave the room. I felt incapable of passing the night alone, so I went to the cafeteria at the end of the corridor. I found several clusters of ashen-faced people there drinking from paper cups of burnt coffee. Those at the nearest tables caught my eye and nodded as I sat down before resuming their somber whispering.

I struggled for weeks to compose the letter, eventually coming to the conclusion that the most important thing was just to write it. By that point my extended internet research had generated an image of my father that was frozen in time. The available biographies were a brief list of proper nouns—the place he was born, the schools he'd attended, the two movies he'd directed. In all the photographs he wore a stylish (for the decade) Western suit, paired with the same thick black glasses and disarming smile. From this I imagined him as a slightly rakish intellectual, now gray haired and laugh lined but no less prone to the intensity clearly visible in his youth.

I assumed he'd be wondering, first, how I'd managed to find him. I worked for a large media organization and had availed myself of the maximum extent of its resources, though I knew many reporters had tried similar tactics in the past and had failed. I admitted that I'd had the benefit of my mother's inside knowledge, including at least some of my father's favored aliases and a place he'd mentioned offhandedly, decades ago, that he'd have loved to run away to forever. It was a short letter, and in the final lines I relayed, in a matter-of-fact tone, the news I was writing to share.

What I didn't tell him: ten years ago, my mother brought me to Mumbai on some unexpressed nostalgic impulse, perhaps a desire to frequent her old stomping grounds, though everyone she knew and loved in the area had already moved away. We rented a flat near Juhu Beach and every morning took a walk along the shoreline. We rolled our churidars up to our knees to wade in the shallow waves, trying not to think of how filthy the water was. From passing vendors we purchased all manner of snacks—roasted corn and bhel puri and samosas that burned the roof of my mouth. For those few hours, facing the sea, I stopped believing there was an entire city behind us.

When we returned to the flat, we'd flip through the hundreds of satellite channels, the dozens of languages in which programming was offered. We'd spent many nights in our Queens apartment in exactly the same fashion. One afternoon I idly selected a film that was described as a tale of star-crossed lovers who'd met in a number of their past lives as several different creatures but, of course, had not known it. We watched the entire movie, which took us well into dusk. During the intermission we got up to close the windows on the eager mosquitos that had begun to swarm in.

My mother, throughout this time, said nothing. She didn't speak until the director's name rolled up in the credits, while I was still weeping at the movie's heart-rending conclusion.

He directed my movie, too, she said. Though everyone says this one is better.

I could express no opinion on this as I'd never seen her movie; she'd told me it had been a very small production and copies no longer existed. At that moment, though, the power went out and we shrieked and ran around searching for candles in sticky cabinets and stubborn drawers. In the morning I still wanted to talk about the film, and we did— then and many times after. But we always focused on the story, and the director's choices never factored into it.

I returned to work a month after my mother's death, requesting a far-flung assignment to help clear the shroud that had settled over my brain. I craved the control that would come in researching and putting a story together.

The magazine sent me to the Arctic Circle to see if I could replicate the experience of a famed mirage. I flew first to the Lofoten Islands, where I intended to spend a few days interviewing local fishermen. I stayed in a one-room cottage overlooking a narrow inlet lined with boats. The cottage's siding betrayed its former coat of paint, peeling in small, yellow patches with cheerful resilience. From the porthole-shaped kitchen window, I could see wooden fish-drying racks dotting the landscape, looking like the ghostly remnants of a once-bustling tent city.

I called the friend looking after my apartment every day, tracking footsteps across the morning's blank slate of fresh snow as I searched for a spot with sufficient cell reception. My friend seemed alarmed by my persistent requests to check the mailbox, which I begged her to do even on Sundays when we both knew the postal service did not deliver. In all that time, though, no letter arrived, and all of my questions about my father persisted.

I felt lucky to have the distraction of work, the distraction of the landscape. The mountains on the islands were whittled into sheer cliff faces that rose from the sea like megalithic ancient gods. In the face of this scale, all signs of civilization—houses, humans, ships—looked toy sized. Speaking with the fishermen, I caught quite a bit of this sense of awe. It seemed entirely plausible that you could encounter a wave you might mistake for a mountain, that the sea could encounter a human it might mistake for a plaything.

My assignment was rooted in an explorer's nineteenth-century expedition to find a route through the Arctic Ocean that would form an essential part of the Northwest Passage. Off the coast of Greenland, the explorer stood on the deck of his ship looking at the horizon, seeking a way through the surrounding icebergs. In the midst of the ice he glimpsed a long range of mountains running from one end of the bay to the other. He sketched the range and named the peaks and then ordered the ship to turn around. The next year a fellow explorer returned to the same spot and, seeing no mountains, sailed straight on through.

After the Lofotens I flew on to Nuuk, where I enlisted a crew to help me sail to the location of the explorer's infamous vision. I had never slept as well as those nights at sea, my cabin akin to a gently rocking womb. During the day, though, I clung like a barnacle to the deck's railing, wondering when the violent waves would finally chop up our vessel and devour it. My photographer looked miserable, his seasickness bands so tight they seemed to be cutting off blood circulation to his hands.

We reached the spot without much difficulty and the captain let us stay there for several days, unworried about becoming trapped in encroaching ice, given the unseasonable warmth. Every few hours I returned to the deck and scanned the horizon. The term for a sailor's mirage—fata morgana—is named for a sorceress of Arthurian legend who was believed to create images of castles in the sky that lured sailors to their demise. I thought of sirens and Mother Nature, how simple misfortune comes to be labeled a complex bewitching; how the only illusions I'd ever felt capable of were ones directed at self-preservation.

I don't know if a mirage works if you're expecting it, my photographer said, his eyes also directed at the vanishing point. Though maybe that's our angle.

A few times a seal splashed up from the gray below, its whiskered face regarding us curiously. We ate fish for every meal, even breakfast, and I noticed that icebergs were not pure white at all but comprised of swirling gradations of colors. At night the aurora borealis haunted the skies with trails left by dancing spirits, the kind of magic my mother would have observed slack-jawed, ablaze with burgeoning epiphany. I considered a different angle for my piece, about images by and of parents constructed from thin air, pedestaled statues toppled and replaced with ordinary, fallible humans. In the end I wrote a piece about all the things I actually saw, but the magazine chose to run a photo essay instead. The slideshow—crisp and polished—looked very much like a trip I'd want to take.

An airmailed package arrived the day after I returned. I ripped the envelope open to find my mother's film, a hand-marked DVD in a plastic jewel case. I checked several times, even picking apart the lining, but my father hadn't included a note. I let my anticipation cancel out my disappointment about his silence. Perhaps, I thought, he had sent the film as a means of establishing a shared vocabulary for a future conversation.

A Place of Ghosts, I gathered, was based on an old legend. My mother's first appearance on the screen, after the credits, lifted every hair and opened every scab on my body. She plays a seventeenth-century princess living in a sprawling stone fortress at the foot of a tree-covered mountain. Her beauty attracts all manner of unwanted attention, including that of a charming visitor no one has seen or heard of before. The princess allows the man to woo her, taking long walks with him around the fort's extensive grounds and discussing philosophical questions with him by lotus-filled pools. It is readily apparent in the film that the princess has fallen in love with the man, and I can't tell whether my mother is acting. Her eyes go wide, she smiles at wayward comments, she seems to move about her surroundings in a personal bubble of bliss. The intimacy evident in her expression made it seem like one I should not have been privy to.

The princess agrees to marry the man, and wedding arrangements get underway. The night before the wedding, the princess strolls with the man in the gardens, fragrant with night-blooming flowers. She begins to feel light-headed, and the man asks if he can fetch her something to drink. She agrees, but as soon as he crosses a tall hedge, passing out of her sight, she realizes she would rather just turn in early given the lengthy festivities that will commence the next day. She heads back toward the palace to find the man and bid him good night. Not ten paces down the path she spots his tall form, crouched over a carved wooden table. He is muttering incantations and crushing herbs to pour into a silver cup etched with her initials, the same one he had gifted her upon his arrival.

Here, the camera lingers on a closeup of my mother's moonlit face, tracking the slow dawning of her realization, the trajectory of emotions between expectant joy and sudden grief. She grows livid, understanding that the man has been using dark magic to court her. She throws a heavy rock at him that by chance misses high and dislodges the cornerstone of the decorative arch the man is standing under. The arch crumbles loudly, flattening him. From the rubble she hears a few phrases of hoarse chanting, which she recognizes as an ancient curse for her home city to be destroyed.

The film ends with the princess standing atop a high, crenellated tower, watching the approach of an invading army that vastly outnumbers her own kingdom's forces. The final shot is of my mother's face, showing her looking not defeated but defiant. Over the credits we learn that the ghosts of both the princess and her dark-hearted suitor are said to still haunt the ruined fort together.

The unknown number that had been calling me at inopportune times turned out to be an estate lawyer, bearing what purported to be my mother's will and final wishes. When I finally caught the call and answered, I took so long to respond after he introduced himself that he assumed I'd hung up. Hello? Are you there? he kept asking, while I adjusted myself to the voice I was hearing: a lawyer calling from only a few blocks away, instead of my father across the oceans and decades I'd imagined. I agreed to meet him at his office on Roosevelt Avenue, which turned out to be only a short walk from the first apartment my mother and I had lived in. I settled myself in an imitation Chesterfield chair and stared at the wall behind him, lined with thick leather-bound books.

I tried to picture myself behind his long mahogany desk, drumming my fingers on its surface and sizing up a steady stream of clients. I felt no regret for having quit law school after only one year. What I'd loved about the law had always been its sense of possibilities—of fairness, justice, equity—but this had never seemed to manifest in what I'd learned or practiced. My mother, though, had wrung her hands at my decision and shouted at me not to throw my life away. Her years as a secretary for a series of men with framed degrees on the wall had convinced her of certain routes to success, even as she herself rejected rigid rules and ways of thinking. I regret that we didn't speak then for nearly a year, the first major rift in our otherwise tightly bound relationship. When I finally returned to the house, conciliatory bouquet of tulips in hand, I found a folder in a kitchen drawer that contained every article that had run with my byline in the intervening months.

After a few pleasantries, the lawyer read out the document, which was brief and pertinent only in that it designated a place for my mother's ashes to be scattered. He squinted his eyes as he reached the name. Gol-con-da Fort, he said, drawing out the syllables as if the mere arrangement of letters in the word were suspect. That mean something to you? I nodded, putting together that this fort must have long ago been used, via unofficial channels, as a very low-cost filming location. The worry lines in the lawyer's forehead smoothed out and he steepled his fingers, leaning toward me. Well, he said, that's all the instructions she left me with. If there's anything else I can do—

I'll confess I had hoped for something more, though I didn't reveal this to the lawyer. After all, my mother and I had kept secrets: I wanted a safe of treasures, a cache of documents, a library of thumbed-through books. In lieu of her life, I wanted anything she had quietly produced. But there was nothing other than the slip of paper with the instructions, not even written in her hand. The lawyer saw me hesitating in the doorway and offered to make me a copy of the document, thinking I needed to note down the place to remember it. His confusion heartened me, as it put me back in the position of knowing something more about my mother than he did.

As I walked home, I passed a pet store and remembered how, during childhood, I'd begged my mother for a turtle that I could keep in a little glass terrarium. My mother encouraged this obsession only to the extent of gamely ferrying me to the nearest pet store, where I could visit the turtles without ever bringing one home. They each had thin yellow lines crisscrossing their backs, like paths to places I'd never been but would instantly recognize. One day at the store, I noticed a printed placard that labelled the reptiles as "False Map Turtles." The sign had a bulleted list of facts underneath, which included that the signature maps fade when the turtles age into adulthood, leaving only a plain, green-black shell. After that, I stopped asking my mother for a turtle, for any pet, unable to stomach the future dimming of my youthful fantasies. I cultivated a healthy sense of fear about the things that could be lost to the years.

∾

Back at my apartment I searched for flights to India, shuddering at the layovers I'd have to endure for a cheaper ticket. I hadn't been back since the Mumbai trip with my mother a decade earlier, money and time having long been too tight for transatlantic jaunts. Going all that way also made it seem necessary to try to see my father. I didn't know how the man would compare to the amorphous idea he was in my head; I wasn't sure if this was a measure I truly wanted to take. But I still felt simultaneously rootless and weighted by the information my mother had imparted. I couldn't see any other way to resolve the situation than to stand before him, be faced with the fact of him. I composed another letter to my father while the airline processed my payment.

Booked, I said, to the silver urn atop my bookcase.

I recognized the impulse behind my mother's final wishes even if I didn't fully understand them. I could have guessed that she wouldn't have chosen the traditional scattering in a holy river; she had never been very religious. We'd observed major festivals out of a sense of duty or culture rather than a fervent sense of belief. She'd placed her faith, instead, in the invisible hand that lay behind what appeared as chance and coincidence.

My mother had visited right after I'd moved out of our apartment and into a cramped one-bedroom in Astoria, eager to double-check the quality of my new-found independence. Though I hadn't moved far (relative, for instance, to the distance she herself had traveled away from her own parents), the few miles loomed like a gulf compared to the block-long radius we'd operated within in Jackson Heights. I'd given my mother a quick tour of my apartment, noticing that she was quietly taking in the contents. After the walk-through, she asked whether I had considered vastu, which, of course, I hadn't; I'd never heard her mention any of the principles, nor had I made place for an ancient feng shui–like system in my life. When she began elaborating, though, I recognized that the apartment I'd grown up in, the apartment she now lived in alone—all of these spaces were organized in accordance with the same principles, so subtly harmonious I'd never noticed. I followed her into my bedroom, where she wanted to reverse the location of my bed because the headboard was pointed north. Even with the two of us pushing, we couldn't move the heavy teak frame a single inch.

In the end she simply moved my stack of pillows to the foot of the bed. You are alive with your own magnetic forces, she said, so you should point your body in a direction to attract good energy, not repel it. I teased her about the piles of dormant dust she seemed to believe were within us, waiting to revolt upon an improper orientation. But even after she left—even though it was uncomfortable to accidentally kick my feet every night against the solid headboard, even though I outwardly scoffed at her unprovable tenets of spirituality—I never moved my pillow back. There are things we don't know unless we are told; there are things we continue to tell ourselves. It became comforting to think of my body quivering like a compass needle, retaining some marrow-deep way of knowing true north.

At the top of Golconda Fort the air was stifling. The pigeons roosting did not stir; they watched the lake, which, from a certain angle, looked flat and unceasing like an ocean. From that height the Buddha statue in the center of the waters could have been the slim mast of a ship. The day was overcast with smog, and the exact line between lake and sky was difficult to discern. Centuries earlier, the Dutch East India Company had come this far inland and still drawn up maps with a spine of nonexistent mountains running down the center of the subcontinent. The trick of a mirage being: it is never impossible, just unreal.

I wandered the grounds, clambering over boulders into off-limit areas no guard was around to whistle me out of. I climbed until I found a stretch of dilapidated walls running along a cliff that I recognized from my mother's film. The scrubby ground was littered with candy wrappers, plastic soda bottles, and cigarette butts, but there was no one else in sight. From a patch behind the wall I collected a bouquet of wildflowers that seemed to wilt as soon as they were plucked. I said a few words and watched the ashes catch the light breeze, particles dispersing on the hillside below. I tucked the urn back into my knapsack and returned to the well-trodden tourist paths, where I was immediately accosted by a vendor selling postcards of the site. If he noticed that my eyes were red and my cheeks tear-stained, he did so after it was already too late to back out of the interaction. I bought a card at random, shoving it in my pocket without looking at it, hoping it didn't say *Wish You Were Here!*

My letter about visiting my father had gone unanswered, but I hailed a taxi straight to the airport. The trip was already planned, and I did not want to linger in a place where it seemed all too easy to stumble into or onto a past life. It was easier to keep going. Stopping to consider would force me to confront my misgivings, determine whether closure rested in seeing or not seeing his face as it was now. What had my mother expected me to do? Was such knowledge imparted as a means of closing or opening a loop?

The flight to Bagdogra was an uneventful two and a half hours, though when we arrived it felt I had landed in a different country. I had only known an India of hot plateaus and humid beaches, not the fresh, brisk air of the north. From Bagdogra I hired a jeep and driver to take me the additional three hours to Darjeeling. It was both easier and more difficult to get there than I'd imagined. It felt a bit like my father had been hiding all these years in plain sight.

I knew the town was a hill station but had not been prepared for how steep the drive was. At times it seemed we were straining upward at a seventy-five-degree angle. I held my breath each time the driver shifted gears, fearing that something wouldn't catch and we would go plummeting backward into the clouded valley below. The air grew cooler and cooler, and when the driver stopped for an afternoon chai, I popped the trunk to get to my suitcase, pulling out the thick sweater I'd never unpacked after my trip to the Arctic Circle.

It was late afternoon when I arrived at my hotel. I fell straight into bed, cranking up the space heater until

I stopped shivering. My flight back was scheduled for the following afternoon, which did not afford much time for the appropriate summoning of will. In the vanity mirror I examined my features: my mother's eyes, the nose and mouth I'd been carrying around all this time from my father's face. I practiced the questions I wanted to ask, saying them over and over again with different inflections until the words lost all meaning.

The next morning, before dawn, I woke and asked my driver to take me to Tiger Hill, a lookout point for the Himalayas where I hoped to catch a glimpse of Mount Kanchenjunga and, if I was lucky, Mount Everest. I arrived in pitch darkness, using my phone's flashlight to follow the dirt path leading up from the parking lot. The sunrise grew outward from the faintest pinprick of light. The shifts in color, extending across the sky in gradient bands, were imperceptible when stared at directly, only becoming obvious when they registered in my peripheral vision. Eventually, I blinked, and the landscape was filled with radiant daylight. I heard someone gasp and scanned the horizon desperately. Just clouds, said a passing vendor, though none of the tourists stopped videotaping.

How easy, I thought, for the right arrangement of vapor to trick the eye into seeing a mountain. I'd been waiting for months for a response from my father that made some acknowledgement of his paternity, but he'd kept himself ungraspable, out of reach. All he'd sent me was my mother: the parent who'd raised me, the woman who linked my father and me via lives kept separate with no overlap. I realized now that she had offered me his name as a fact to correct a record already written, of which he'd been no part. He had offered me the film as a means of staying the director, the man my mother once knew. There was no sense in my trying to prove the mirage of his fatherhood real when its power rested in illusion, in fantasy. Beneath it was the same landscape as it always had been.

Still, I kept waiting for the morning mist to burn off, long after the sun would have cleared the day had it wished to do so. My driver paced behind me, growing grumpy as the vendors ran out of coffee and increasingly anxious about the time. At ten he tapped me on the shoulder, pointing at his watch and saying we needed to leave immediately to make the visit I'd told him about, to my father's house. The roads are not good, miss, he said, it will take some time to get there and then you have to catch your flight. I made no move to get up. I wished I could have asked my mother whether she'd ever come here, whether the elements had cooperated for her. My other questions seemed suddenly insignificant. Any answers my father might give were unanchored, already floating away.

Only one stop, I told the driver, noting his expression of relief.

We left for the airport midmorning. When the clouds finally parted, they revealed only a dense thicket of fog.

The Peak of
Eternal Light

I didn't miss the moon, not at first. I grew used to seeing the Earth, instead: a weighted marble that never rolled to the horizon. I was relieved I hadn't been sent to the dark side, where my home planet never turned its face. I had the privilege of witnessing the seas swallow the continents, the creeping film of smog smudge out my birthplace.

There were days—monthlong days—when my iridescent suit refused to fasten flush with my helmet and my plants preferred to wilt rather than rise into a manufactured atmosphere. When my cinderblock-simple housing structure looked less like a technological marvel and more like a child's failed science project. And still the view beyond remained a churn of blue and brown, evidence of forces engaged in a struggle to control the Earth's surface, ones that since unleashed could no longer be steered or managed by humans. I wondered how different the planet would look from this vantage point when the waves and toxic clouds finally claimed it for themselves.

But: even and especially on such days I felt necessary. As the one-person maintenance crew my space agency had kept on the moon, I was the sole caretaker for a fledgling lunar colony I'd helped envision. The heady initial months of construction were carried out by nonscientists, a crew of energy sector mercenaries who'd snaked water pipelines from crater-bottom ice to the massifs, and installed fields of solar panels to take advantage of the near-constant light at the southern pole. I'd arrived to the aftermath. I was unused to seeing civilian infrastructure without any sign of humans. My first thought was that the place already looked like ruins, though everything was brand new.

My second was: god, this impossible place, its shape, its scale.

Over time I learned to actively push away the rest. Don't think about the 272 days you've spent here alone, waiting for the agency to solve the economic problem of mass Earth-to-moon transit and the ethical problem of who would populate the colony. Don't think about how quiet it is in space, where the sound of your own body can drive you mad.

Try to think about survival, your own and everyone else's.

From a young age my face had been always turned up to the heavens. My mother clucked at the bruises that crept across my kneecaps from ground-level objects I never saw coming. But in those blooming stretches of purple and yellow and blue I saw not misfortune but a miracle—a microcosm of the cosmos unfurled on my own skin.

In our village back then people died from the usual causes but also from mysterious coughs that worsened instead of going away, strange rashes that spread outward from the chest, and sips of water that permanently closed the throat. The school's headmistress pushed anyone with near-decent marks, even girls, to become doctors. Put your skills to use in the much-needed area of healing, she told me. We have to figure out what's happening and how to fix it.

Our calendar was lunisolar. Because the moon and sun don't keep the same time, every so often Adhik Maas was added to the primarily lunar calendar for alignment. This extra thirteenth month was considered an inauspicious period—not the time to embark on anything new or momentous. Instead, we turned inward, praying and fasting and trying to perform good deeds. We were meant to take advantage of the boon of time: a chance to be the person we hadn't been, or the person we still hoped to be, in all the other months of the year. I used it to study celestial bodies and their movements, to draw up wild fantasies of life on other planets that might have the possibility of being put into practice.

By the time I was 10, my mother was placing a mask over my nose and mouth each morning and securing its elastic bands behind my ears. So was every other kid's parent or older sibling, all of whom then fit a slightly larger mask on themselves directly after. A cottage industry soon sprouted around mask design, with some enterprising locals selling ones emblazoned with superheroes, Bollywood stars, and dead politicians. Mine had a miniature solar system, which I'd crudely drawn with colored markers, adding a tiny blue speck for forlorn nonplanet Pluto.

Already at that age I sensed the world was not long for us, that there was no point in curing diseases that would only multiply and persist. I regarded the stars as an uncommon but legitimate calling, a worthy means of fixing a growing problem.

What other solution, when living on Earth was what was killing us?

❧

The agency's first lunar probe, named after the moon god, Chandra, was launched the year I was born. Our country became the fourth to plant its flag on the moon, and our leaders touted success with nationalistic fervor. My mother gave birth in a crowded hospital where the only televisions were in common waiting areas. The speeches and commentators droned in the background as my grandmother knit a small pink hat in her lap, expectant of her own good news.

Later, perhaps in school, I learned that the probe's most significant discovery was evidence of water ice. Water, as in: elixir of life, possibility of habitation. The probe's spectrometers mapped minerals and broken water molecules; subsequent probes tested soil samples and recorded moonquakes. The agency learned what it wanted to about the lunar landscape before growing bored and moving on to farther bodies. In files and drawers, a shadow topography was stored. Shadow, as in: blueprint for another life, possibility of a parallel existence.

❧

Humans are primed for sudden change, but uninhabitability was a gradual process. Like the frog jumping out when placed in boiling water but sitting in a pot of cold water heating slowly, noticing too late the rolling bubbles.

The year I joined the agency, my colleagues were gripped with only a vague sense of panic. Their actions were not yet frantic. Bengaluru—set deep in the V of the subcontinent as it narrowed to its ocean-facing point—felt exactly the distance it was from the country's international borders. Those entry points were just beginning to clog with climate refugees. The innovations we relied on made daily life in the city seem manageable, made it possible to forget or avoid confronting the country's true condition. The agency's ambit was exploration on a time-scale of generations. I was more than happy to design and send off probes for planets they would not reach in even a granddaughter's lifetime.

By my third year, the smog was growing exponentially. It expanded and stalked those fleeing until it covered even the last patch of blue sky. Borders closed and people flows halted. There was nowhere to look in the gray haze. At sunrise and sunset, it tinged orange, at night, blue-black. That steady progression felt like a reminder of the universe's continued functioning beyond the killing air. The country's gaze drifted, panicked, until it landed on those of us in the agency: a proxy for what was unseen but still hoped to be out there.

Those who could afford it began to trade make-shift masks for sealed personal air filtration devices, which wrapped around the head. Around election times, painted lorries would drive out to rural areas and drop off boxes of devices with the customary bags of rice. Soon enough there was sufficient pressure to make the devices near free of cost and widely available, accomplished by classifying them as a life-saving device. They were worn all day, even indoors. You never knew if someone might have left a window cracked open, or a door somewhere in the vicinity ajar.

Special soft, pillow-padded versions of the device were released for sleeping, and all models had a small revolving door-style portal around the mouth for eating and drinking. We relied on our self-driving transport to take us wherever we needed to go, because walking even with a device on was a useless proposition with visibility hovering constantly at near zero.

The smog existed in simultaneous states: it appeared as air, filled in all empty space between Earth and sky like liquid, and choked the body like a solid. In time, the ultimate act of intimacy became to let another person touch your face.

※

Lunar regolith is a surprisingly durable material. I printed all the tools I needed. The buildings I lived and worked in, such as my residence, the printing shed, the grow houses, and the control room, were fitted with gravity-controlling chambers. These simulated Earth's conditions so that I didn't suffer too much bone and muscle-mass loss during my tenure on the moon. I had no mirror, so I could only hope to catch a stray reflection in an extra helmet. Or look down at my own body, pinching the skin and wondering whether I was wasting away.

Whatever we were constructing, it was not a duplicate Earth. The unremitting gray of life here—crafted wholesale from dust, like sandcastles—made it impossible to ever forget my presence on the moon.

Moreover: there was no atmosphere, no weather. I suppose this could have been considered a respite from the situation on Earth, a true blank slate to build from. But try to envision a tableau without clouds, without sky. I had nowhere to aim my thoughts, my imagination. For a time I lost perspective altogether. I hadn't realized I regarded the sky as a gauge or a safe barrier. How it bleached around a sea, weighted before a storm, sparkled with the air's crispness.

Here my suit and structures were all aimed at protecting me from the moon's wild temperature swings. The surface was like a desert, fluctuating between freezing and boiling depending on the time of day and how much sun reached the surface. But I was maintained at lukewarm, and whether it was cold or hot outside, I could never tell the difference.

Uninhabitability was a gradual process. My womb grew increasingly stubborn and painful fibroids until my doctor suggested a hysterectomy. I was relatively young and otherwise healthy, she said; recovery would be quick given recent advances. I told her to set up the operation.

I'd scheduled the appointment during a lunch break, because I'd just started at the agency and was wary of taking time for personal matters. The car synced to my calendar and knew where to go without my having to ask. After, it began to return to the office, weaving through leafy, narrow backstreets to avoid congestion on the broader avenues. At some point I registered where we were going—at that time it was still possible to glimpse surroundings through the windows—and gave a manual override command to stop. This never resulted in an immediate halt but rather a careful process of the car seeking the nearest curb, similar to pulling over when called to by flashing police lights.

Several hundred feet later, after a row of scooters and rickshaws had darted around, the car settled against a cracked stretch of sidewalk. The walkway ringed a small park, which in turn surrounded a reservoir filled with water of a dubious color for human consumption.

Inside the park I sat on a metal bench beneath a tree in riotous bloom. Every so often it dropped yellow trumpet-shaped flowers around me, as if it would continue to present offerings until it felt I sufficiently appreciated them. The park was empty save for a few groups of salwar-clad speed-walking women huffing visibly beneath their masks. They nodded once for each lap as they passed.

I thought of the look of sympathy in my doctor's eyes, how she'd grabbed and squeezed my hand before I'd left the room. You can still have children, you know, she'd said, quietly, as if letting me in on a secret. There are so many wonderful adoption agencies, if you want I can give you some names—

The look had morphed quickly when I told her I'd already decided, before the fibroids ever appeared, not to have children. Even as a teenager I'd sensed a ticking clock, the feeling of an approaching countdown.

I was familiar with the doctor's expression of pity. She worked all day with women's bodies and had developed a certain understanding of both their function and purpose. On her desk sat a framed family photo, she and her husband posing with a daughter each on their knees, both girls in pigtails and matching lehengas and full-face grins.

I wondered which of that family, if any, would be granted passage off the planet if and when the lunar colony I'd envisioned was set up. The agency had hired me because of a lunar colony model I'd mocked up in my previous job at an aerospace company. The model had won the company a lucrative future contract if the colony was ever pursued. More importantly, it earned me a meagerly paying government position, but one that might eventually allow me to realize a dream of going to space. My early drafts of the largest eventual version of the colony envisioned a capacity of no more than a thousand people. That number could easily have been one family's wedding guest list.

Another trumpet flower fell by my sneaker, the petals wilted and closed around a set of bent pistils. In the depths of my purse, I found an extra shoelace. I entwined the dropped flowers and shoelace until they formed a makeshift garland, small and child-sized, which I left on the bench. As I reached my car I saw the speed-walkers stop in an upset huddle by that spot. They were looking around to see who'd left the garland so they could demand why, determine whether it had been placed there to ring the neck of a god or a ghost. Finding no one around to answer, they backed away slowly from the bench and dispersed.

The agency and I communicated via regular transmissions, but once a week we had an almost-live (with three-second lag) video call. I suited up to walk to the control room, which was another one-room regolith structure distinguishable only for the tall, silver antenna crowning its roof like a steeple. If some other beings tried to decipher the ruins of this colony, I imagined them tagging this building a religious place.

I listened to the commander's update. Still major problems of funding and sending additional personnel, still some problems of load on the rockets, the same problem of deciding civilian inhabitants. I listed the minor issues of the week, the plans I needed sent to print a new can opener. I didn't mention I'd broken the last one myself, that I'd gone to open a can of beans and felt suddenly and irrevocably overcome with helplessness, that I could no longer prevent myself from hearing the tide beating against my eardrums and the steady thumping of my own heart, the only sounds that were there to keep me company. Before I could quell the impulse, I'd flung the opener against the regolith wall of my residence. When I went to examine the damage, the utensil had cracked open at its hinge but I could find no evidence of the impact on the wall, not even a tiny chip.

The commander didn't dwell further on the can opener, for which I was grateful. He moved into an overview of other countries' progress with their colonies. I knew most countries—and a few corporations—had decided to build near the poles, where there had been some evidence of water and more favorable climate conditions. Most were using the moon as a practice run for farther and more inhabitable planets, including ones yet to be discovered.

The commander mentioned that the Americans were sending a manned mission that was due to arrive the following week. I tried not to look too eager. The American colony was located at the same pole as ours, and the pole's shared landing base was not far from the outer reaches of our colony. Outside of shared spaces like landing areas, travel between the actual colonies was difficult and frowned upon, as there were quite a few hush-hush research projects being enacted within their borders.

You can greet him at the landing base as a gesture of goodwill, he continued, though I was already planning to do so, with or without the commander's permission. It had been so long since I'd experienced the physical presence of another person.

He sent a picture and a bearded man's face filled the screen, posed in front of an American flag. I recognized the name beneath first, for I hadn't seen this man since childhood. The details of his face resolved into a more aged version of the lanky boy I'd known. His family had left and emigrated to the U.S. when we were both 10, and after that we'd lost touch.

∾

In childhood we'd talked frequently of becoming astronauts. For a number of reasons, not the least of which was my gender, it had seemed more probable then for him.

We hadn't lived close to each other. He was the son of a prominent scientist and came from a moneyed part of town that once housed the orchards for a local king's palace. I came from an area of streets of one-storied houses built solely for practicality, without any architectural flourishes. But from the age of 10 we went to the same school, in a sort of liminal zone between our neighborhoods where it was possible for children as different as ourselves to meet.

He first spoke to me when we were 12, when I beat him on a math test, when the score I'd earned was perfect and the teacher announced it to the whole class as such. He complimented the solar system-covered mask I was wearing as we waited in front of the school to catch an auto-rickshaw home. I complimented the intricate detail in the drawing of Saturn and its rings he'd done on his. From then on we spent most afternoons together, inventing some excuse about extra work to our parents, though this never felt like a lie because our discussions were for the most part scholarly and scientific.

I remembered he could recite the details of planetary bodies like they were friends he knew. And he called them by deity names—Shukra and Surya and Budh and Shani—interspersing celestial legends with facts about seismic and atmospheric details. He told me the gods, seeking an elixir of immortality, once churned an ocean of milk until it spat up all manner of treasures, one of which was the moon. Chandra's body was shining, brilliant, so much so that the gods preferred him to dwell far away in space. Depending on who you ask for a legend, waxing and waning may be explained by Chandra being: emptied and refilled as a cup with life-giving ambrosia for the gods; cursed after an unlucky romantic scenario; or cursed to a withering death but saved at the last moment by his wives, resulting in a reprieve that made him whole to be parceled out, over and over again.

I remembered he also told me "graha" meant "planet" in Sanskrit, in the sense of that body seizing or influencing the destiny of mankind. But I could never summon the faith he might have felt, because it was a power that felt ill-placed. What if the power were instead in our hands? What if we chose not to abuse it? I thought of how an orbit might be the blink of an eyelid for some god but a thousand lifetimes for a human.

In childhood you can have a best friend for an hour, for a day, for a month, and then you never see them again. I had one for about a year, before his father accepted a teaching post abroad and just like that, he was gone, and the afternoons stretched out empty once more.

∿

I'd only really learned to drive a scooter before self-driving cars became ubiquitous. My lunar vehicle, though, was manual. I felt the sluggishness of my reflexes, how I hesitated in turning the wheel and missed dodging several significant bumps in the terrain. Driving felt harrowing, and even after I noticed my knuckles turning white, I didn't loosen my grip on the wheel.

I wondered how long we could reasonably spend catching up before he would have to set out for the American colony. I wasn't sure I even cared about catching up. The information that mattered was communicated by the uniforms we wore, the fact that we were meeting on a distant rock he'd called Chandra, who was the father of Budh, or Mercury. I wanted to hear his voice. I wanted to hear a story without gods or even us in it.

As I crested a steep set of dunes, creeping over the edge with my foot on the brake, I spotted the landing area. It was basically an open area abutted by a few buildings, one of which had been draped with the flag of the Interlunar Agency—a large white circle on a gray background. The buildings housed extra suits and vehicles, repair items, a 3D printer, communication devices, and other equipment.

His rocket already should have been there. The Americans partnered with a private company for transport that prided itself on how quickly it could span the distance between Earth and the moon. I'd timed my arrival for an hour after his scheduled landing time, knowing there were a variety of checks and shutdowns he would need to conduct before he could exit his ship.

It wasn't out of the ordinary, though, for there to have been a short delay. I inched to one of the outer buildings that I knew was a residence pod and settled in to wait.

I sat there for twelve hours, what I might have once called half a day. When I could no longer bear the questions in my mind, I went to the control center to send a querying transmission but found several urgent messages already blaring in red text and all-caps on the screen. They spoke of near accident and averted tragedy, of a fortunate ejection and a parachute-assisted escape.

My friend and I had talked of danger, back in childhood, like it was a necessity. Dismissed it in the way of children relishing the feeling of their own ignited potential, the faint suspicion of adult immortality. Nascent technology carried inherent risk, we'd said, pretend-knowingly. I felt now that we had recognized quite well the problem of space but ignored entirely the problem of time. How little of it there truly was, even if you had prepared yourself for this dwindling. How the future is a concept of relativity, and it matters whether you are the object in motion or the observer.

I read the rest of the transmissions and some news reports. The close call had prompted worldwide investigations and an inquiry into common means and methods.

My space agency's lunar program, as well as similar missions around the world, had been put on indefinite hold until those efforts could be concluded satisfactorily. The commander applauded my sense of duty in a brief message to which he appended "hang in there" as a postscript.

THE ROCKET HAS ACHIEVED LIFTOFF, the penultimate transmission from the Americans said, followed by, THE ROCKET IS NO LONGER COMING.

The drive to the colony went quicker on the way back. I pushed the accelerator toward the floor of the vehicle, slid across spans of gray sand, having nothing to crash into. I felt a bit reckless. I cared less, for a moment, about my own safety. I imagined a breeze in my hair, the weight of no one here and everyone there being lifted. The future would come, I thought, however slowly or quickly. I had faith in that. And in the meantime, I could be the object in motion.

Having no attachments—deceased parents and no partner or offspring—I was considered an ideal candidate for the agency's lunar mission when it finally kicked off, based on my models, in my third year there. I was fast-tracked through astronaut training and then unanimously selected for the maintenance position, to stay on after the initial crew had helped put down the roots of the colony.

For a full year before leaving, as part of a psychological evaluation of sorts, I was asked to keep a dream journal. There are many days I could not remember my dreams and left the pages blank. There are other pages in which I made elaborate drawings instead, a feeble attempt to capture how I'd dreamt of opening my eyes to a different world.

But some dreams I did not write in the journal at all. Like: I took my long-lost friend to visit the constellations that watched over each of us on the nights we were born. I grew gills and learned to breathe water as if it were air. I jet-propelled up to the peak of a nearby mountain, the moon full and bright above me. I stared down at all the people, generations and generations of them milling about on the gently sloping curve of the Earth, which no longer seemed bent back toward destruction.

Bloom

The face of the mountain slid off while we were en route to the yearly miracle. Otherwise, the range was fixed to the horizon ahead like future time— always approaching but never arriving. We trekked day and night to reach our destination, which was located somewhere around the vanishing point. From our homes it was a ten-day journey, all ascent. Leader liked to say it was difficult to indicate this direction properly on a sign. The arrow would very clearly say *up*, but the mind would persist in reading it as *forward*.

Spring had been venturing into the landscape, marking the rocky terrain with green shoots and mud from recent rains. The journey might have been quicker by horse, but only the men were permitted to ride. In our procession the boy children went first on mules, so their view could be unobstructed. The girl children, me among them, walked next with the women, who carried the group's bags and babies. We were followed in the rear by the husbands on horseback. And last, of course, was Leader, the better to watch over us all and ensure no one fell behind.

The bloom would not open until we arrived, but it was not waiting for us. It was a matter of timing. Each year, in mid-March, the petals uncurled from their fetal sleeping positions, stretched out to face the sun. The flower saw all it needed to of the world in a matter of days (in other words, as Leader said, *enough*). When the final petal had wilted and fallen, confettied the rocky outcropping where we knelt together in prayer, we would pack up and leave. But we needed to be there for the unfurling because this was Leader's gift to us. Witnessing was how the men became holy and the women learned to be of service.

After a girl's seventeenth witnessing, she was ready to be wed and to birth children into the embrace of the Leader, which enveloped us all. I was quiet and considered pious, so Leader had promised me to the boy who rode on the first mule. Each year as we journeyed, I studied the back of the boy's head, memorizing the whorl where his black hair came together at a tiny bald spot. I could have drawn that pattern better than the contours of his face. I imagined touching that absence while counting the ninety-nine knots on my belt, silently reciting the names of Leader's forms from each of his past lives, before he achieved his final manifestation in this one. There was an empty space at the end of the braided cotton for the hundredth knot, as in all the girl's belts. It would be tied after my wedding this year, when the boy would finally tell me his true name.

We were still three days from the flower when a distant roar reached us. We did not usually walk single file but sometimes the trail forced us into a queue. We'd just formed a line to travel through the narrow canyon flanked by two steep walls of stone. We remained frozen for several seconds, listening to the sound ricocheting off the walls to our eardrums. The mountain clearing its silted throat, preparing to remove the pit of rock and debris that had lodged there over winter.

Leader spoke often of the ocean, though most of us had never seen it. Like all the children, I'd been born in one of Leader's houses tucked in the valley a week or so's walk away. The flower was the farthest we'd go, we'd ever been. The roar evoked the waves Leader talked about, but the noise only grew louder, without receding. The sound came first, I remember that clearly. Sound first, then the boy's head turned backward, his open mouth, screaming. A chorus of unanswered cries: *Leader, Leader.* The horses' and mules' eyes rolling and their mouths frothing. The women and girls scattering to press against

102 WHERE TO CARRY THE SOUND

the canyon walls, clinging to the rough stone. Then the horses and mules bolted in the direction we'd come. Hot breath from their nostrils seared our skin as they squeezed past, leaving the women and girls on the path. For a few moments we stood in place, waiting for the disaster to arrive. Then from somewhere behind me, I heard a voice calling for us to move, to flee. Around me women were hiking their ankle-length dresses up to their knees to run. The sight of so many bare legs at once was an unbearable intimacy. I'd never seen the scar laddering up my mother's shin before, the butterfly inked on a recent initiate's calf.

A force gripped my wrist and yanked as if aiming to dislocate my shoulder. My head turned to follow my arm and I saw my cousin pulling me along like an obstinate mule. She was running toward a shadow on our left that yawned itself into the mouth of a cave. Inside, the space was as cavernous as our high-raftered gathering hall. Women and girls continued to dart in after us, dropping their jute carrier bags and then collapsing with groans of relief.

The collection of limbs beside me felt familiar, and among the arms and legs I made out the faces of my mother and aunt. There was a disorganized roll call of names cried out at random until everyone had been counted and identified, all twenty of us. A low hum of muttered prayers filled the cave until the barrage outside overtook it. I covered my ears and watched as the darkness become deeper, more absolute.

After some time I began crawling, seeking the well-worn trail. I wondered if once the fear wore off, the horses and mules would run a circle right back to us, return to the weathered hands that had always tended to them. Or if they'd keep running, carry the men and boys to lands I couldn't imagine. I tried to picture the boy on the first mule watching us emerge from the cave, or regarding an unknown expanse. In each case, the face I summoned was expressionless. Like a portrait drawn not from life or memory but from a secondhand account.

As I crawled I felt others creeping next to me, drawn in the same direction. After a short distance, our heads butted against a wall where the cave entrance had been. We stood and touched a solid expanse of stone and packed mud, the mountain's sloughed-off detritus. But it was shaped like a mound and there were soft divots that could serve as handholds. I reached up and climbed until I saw a glimmer of the daylight I knew must still exist. The opening was a crack only wide enough to peer out of while reaching a single hand outside. I could not make sense of what was visible through the opening; the perspective was askew. Every angle looked like the ground. Somewhere above us a river of rock, stone, and mud had been released. Thus freed, it had cascaded wildly down the mountain to fill the canyon.

Back in the darkness, a match was struck, and then another. Faces materialized in the gloom. The women who had been repeating Leader's past forms aloud in unison grew silent. We peered at each other. No one felt compelled to state what was obvious about the omnipresent darkness, that it signaled an utter lack of egress. My aunt sat up after some time and dug through her bag, calling out to the other women who were carrying food supplies. They named each item in their bags. Then the women carrying water named how many sips were left in their canteens. Then how many sticks remained in the matchboxes. Then how many candles. How many prayerbooks. How many tools. How many days till the witnessing. How many scrapes, cuts, and bruises.

For some, the permablack surroundings disrupted the body's rhythms and made it difficult to stay awake. But that night, or what passed for it, I had trouble sleeping. The hours evaporated. I was already prone to sickness at this stage of the journey, this height. The altitude makes your body aware that it is breathing, but I don't think the body likes to remember. I slipped in and out of dreams, not knowing when I was awake. The air was thick with epiphany. I dreamt the women were whispering stories to each other, or else I actually heard them. I sensed my mother's hands emerging from her skirt, spreading wide in a pose of offering. What could she give that had not previously been pressed upon her, on me? She began a story I had never heard before. It felt a time for revelation:

"Once, there was a childless couple that had reached an age at which they could no longer hope for children. They lived in an isolated stone house in the high mountains, where it snowed quite heavily during a certain portion of the year. The couple kept several goats, selling the milk in the nearest village to provide for themselves. On one such trip to the market, the man passed a squat partridge ensnared in a hunter's trap. The bird squawked miserably, and the man felt a twinge of pity for it. The bird was a wholly ordinary partridge—ordinary in the sense that it was like any other partridge, though each partridge possesses a striking swath of stripes and spots that renders it, upon further examination, anything but ordinary. Seized by a momentary impulse, the man opened the trap to free the partridge, which promptly flew away.

"Later that evening, the man and woman were drinking tea by a fire as snow blanketed the mountain. They heard a knock at the door, which was unusual given not only their remote location but also the inclement weather. The woman opened it to a shivering young girl crouched on the doorstep. The couple had never seen her before. The girl told the couple that she was an orphan whose parents had recently been killed in a bitter land dispute. She had been walking for days searching for a hot meal and somewhere she might sleep for a night. The couple immediately brought her into their home and let her warm herself by the fire. They led her to their tiny extra room, fashioned from a kitchen pantry, with a child-sized bed that for many years they had wished to fill.

"One night turned into a week, then a month, and then a year. Finally, the couple made clear that the girl could stay forever if she wanted, as their daughter. The girl was quiet and loving and doted on the couple. As they were now deep into old age, they welcomed the unexpected boon of her company. The girl asked for a few skeins of wool so that she could practice her weaving, which the couple happily provided. She then sat her parents down and told them the only other thing she would ever ask from them was to never enter her room while she was working. The couple thought her weaving must have been a form of communing with her departed family, and out of respect for this, they naturally agreed.

"The girl locked herself in her room for longer and longer periods, but each time she emerged, it was with a tapestry of increasingly spectacular beauty. The tapestries sold in the market for large sums of money, allowing the couple to cease their own difficult labor. For a time the three of them were content. After several months, though, the couple could no longer contain their curiosity. How could such a young girl, they wondered, create objects of such miraculous beauty? One morning, when the girl had locked herself in her room, the couple knelt by the door's keyhole, desperate to behold their daughter's craft.

"As they peered through the keyhole they were shocked to see not a girl in the room but a small partridge with a decimated plumage. They watched as the partridge plucked its own wing and tail feathers to create a shimmering pile of down on the floor. They noticed the large gaps in the tapestry lying in front of the bird and understood, suddenly, that the feathers were what had made the tapestries so dazzling, so unique. Entranced, the couple continued watching until their arthritic knees demanded they change positions. The man cursed under his breath as he tried to straighten his leg and the partridge looked up, startled, spying two pairs of eyes glinting behind the keyhole. It let out a long, low wail, then flapped its wings and jumped out the window. The couple never saw the girl or the bird again."

My mother did not wait for a reaction after finishing her story. I heard the rustling of her skirt as she settled on the ground. I could not see her face but knew she had turned away from me. I felt every step of the short distance between us. Still, a thin thread connected us: the knowledge of what she'd spun out from deep within her, and what it had cost her to reveal this to me. One could give and give of themselves and label the act devotion, though it might equally be called a flaying. One could ask others to let them keep a single secret for themselves— their sacrifices to survive—and have even this request betrayed. And if so: buried deep inside, one might still find an option left. In my whole life, spent at Leader's feet, I'd never known my mother to have any secrets. Nor had I ever dreamt of being charged with guarding such value myself.

Dawn broke with a single beam of sunlight that filtered through the crack and pierced the wall behind me. One of the food carriers opened a bottle of milk whose scent turned the dank cave air sweet and pastoral. We each took a sip, inhaling the scent of the meadows surrounding our houses where our brown cows usually grazed. Another woman passed around a packet of crackers and we each self-rationed, cracking off pieces or taking handfuls of crumbs. I palmed this meager breakfast and crept back to the opening, climbing to the top of the mound. Outside, the exterior looked the same as yesterday. Though perhaps some of the sharp edges had settled into new patterns, like a prism rolled in a palm, revealing different facets with each shift.

From the opening I watched one of the dark rocks dislodge from the canyon wall across from me and fall.

I followed its trajectory but it did not land. Instead, it grew wings and flew up to the opening, perching on the mound covering the cave entrance, directly in front of my face. The crow peered into my eyes and cocked its head, studying my features. I opened my palm and dusted out the remaining crumbs. The bird pecked at them and then turned and flew off, not taking long to exit my limited field of vision.

Down among the women, we wondered aloud what had happened to the Leader, the men. Were they dead, injured? Even if they lived, would they survive without us? I wondered, too, if they had any intention of looking for us. Was Leader already telling a story about our sacrifice? One as sacred as a bloom pushing itself out of the dirt each year, an ending repeated over and over until it formed another beginning.

Though Leader forbid contact with noninitiates, we knew there was a town near our houses that was aware of us. They might send someone to come looking. If not for us in particular, then for survivors in general. Anyone else who might have been on the path to the summit at the time of the landslide. Periodically the women would each take turns climbing the mound and yelling for help through the opening, wary that every time some stones clattered to the canyon floor, and all that returned was her own echo.

When I climbed back to the opening the next time, there was a shiny black button on top of the mound. It looked like the exact button the women sewed as a fastening on all the men's cotton pants. I pulled loose some thread at the end of my belt and tied the button there. It was the size of the broadest part of my thumb, and it was comforting to rub it against my index finger. My mother and aunt kept telling me to count my knots, to recite the names, and I would make the motions but be gripping the button instead. In the darkness the ritual sounded the same. I did not tell my mother or aunt about the crow, nor the button. I did not tell them I could no longer conjure the boy's whorl, sketch the lines on Leader's face. If any other woman had seen anything atop the mound, while calling out to the empty canyon, they said nothing. It was impossible to tell what everyone kept to themselves.

Another time, I found a brass buckle atop the mound that looked like the kind we used to tighten the leather straps that saddled the men's horses. It was night and I only noticed it through a stray gleam in my peripheral vision. I threaded my belt through the buckle so it sat against my waist. The button and buckle had appeared like gifts, but they were given without any direction, any higher purpose. I could do with them as I wished. I could keep them or hurl them into the darkness below. I could recognize their simple, functional beauty or deem them wholly plain and ordinary. I marveled that the giver had asked nothing of me, not even to notice or accept their offerings. Leader would have offered a sermon about such tokens, but he was not here to deliver it. The resulting blankness in my head was unnerving. But it grew as I sat holding the objects, started to become companionable. The new silence held.

I fell asleep there, curled against the top of the mound. I dreamt of the partridge, a now featherless bird that kept trying to fly but sailed instead into gnarled, naked branches, having nothing left for itself or to give away. I dreamt the crow was Leader in another form, swooping in to assure us he was still watching. I dreamt of the strongest power I could imagine, flight. A pair of wings sprouted from my shoulder blades, but no amount of flapping would lift my feet off the ground. When I woke, I found that the buckle, pressed against my stomach during the night, had imprinted itself on my belly. I was surprised the skin there was still malleable, stretched thin as it was from hunger.

And so we continued, pressing on somehow in the cave. We told time the old way, by the movement of sun and shafts of light. We learned to navigate with our eyes closed, moving through the colorful ribbons that danced against the backs of our eyelids. We finished the milk, half the water, all the crackers. We burned the prayerbooks for light and warmth. We sat in darkness to not use any more matches. We conserved our energy until there was no more left in reserve.

Outside, on a ledge high above us, the flower would have bloomed by now, if it had not been crushed beneath the falling rubble. The crimson petals would still have opened and fallen in our absence. I pictured the unfurling in my mind, how it might look with no crowd gazing upon it, no chorus of sacred song. No one to commemorate the bloom's reemergence, to recognize the very same flower that, in another lifetime, was plucked to close the loop of a garland placed by Leader's betrothed around his neck. And Leader's neck in this life: bare, unadorned, the skin liver-spotted and wrinkled. Riddled like any other person of a certain age with signs of human frailty.

It was possible, I knew, that the flower's blooming had been witnessed. And after, its fallen petals might have shriveled and been ground beneath the heel of a person who knew nothing of Leader. A person who lived unburdened by another man's past lives and the weight of the stories he'd accumulated in them. A person who had taken a walk with no intention other than to stretch their legs, who had by chance reached the top at the perfect moment to look upon a flower blossoming before sinking into the melt. That alone seemed worthy of wonder.

There is a ring we wear when we are betrothed. It is a thin gold band given to us by the Leader at birth, kept safe until engagement and resized for the hands we'd grown into. My fingers had become bone-slender, and it was difficult to keep the band on. I was spending more and more time at the opening because it was taxing to keep climbing up and down. The women rarely moved at all anymore, and I felt reluctant even to call out to them, fearing I'd get no response. Once a day I placed a finger beneath my mother, aunt, and cousin's noses, holding my own breath as I did so.

One evening I climbed to the opening, thinking this might be one of the last times I could make it to the top of the mound. I wanted to look at the stars and reimagine what life looked like on the outside. I wanted to be caressed again by the silence, let it fill slowly with only my mother's story, my own idle thoughts. Above the canyon wall just a sliver of sky was visible. I could see the moon, the night held together by a single, crescent fingernail. After some time I noticed that my ring had slipped off my finger, but I did not reach immediately to put it back on. I wondered if this was a sign of weakness, a failing. But oh, it shined so beautifully in the dirt.

I fell asleep and when I woke with sunrise, the ring was gone. In its place was a slim, silver whistle we used sometimes to call in the herding dogs from the fields. I remembered the noise it produced was sharp and could be heard from quite a distance away. Sometimes even the townspeople's dogs would bark and come running until Leader chased them off. I had barely any breath left. But I blew and blew and blew, naming to the wind where to carry the sound.

In The Forest
of the Night

The hunt has been going on for weeks when she arrives; by then it has already produced a supreme court case and a quasi-military operation. Ria has read about it in international papers and watched breathless local television coverage, the anchor's face nearly covered by stacked chyrons screaming *man-eater* and *still on the loose*. But the atmosphere in her grandmother's village reflects none of the media's mounting hysteria. Rather, she finds the place unbearably solemn, its few shop-lined streets empty of cars, carts, and people.

It is nearing the end of monsoon season, and a downpour soundtracks her first day in the village. From Nani's veranda Ria watches fat droplets form rivers across the cracked pavement. She can barely make out the buildings opposite through the thick veil of water. Visibility in the nearby forest—tangled with fresh growth—must be even worse, any flash of a telltale black-and-orange pelt shrouded by sodden vines and leaves.

The rains break in the evening, just before dusk. Ria and Nani walk to the edge of the village, where slender teak trees begin to crowd and the earth smells like damp sawdust. The true scale of the forest cannot be grasped from this vantage point, nor the increasing number of areas slashed out to accommodate highways, factories, and farms. From here the forest looks like an unbroken swath, and Ria feels it looming like the vast, living mass it is.

They join a few neighbors who have assembled in informal vigil, peering down the dirt path for signs of the hunt team's return. The unseen presence of the hunters—somewhere out there—provides a false sense of security, though those gathered are skeptical about the team's chances of success. The villagers clearly put more faith in Nani, expressing their suspected belief that her new involvement in the hunt, which Ria is assisting, will surely result in the tigress's capture.

Ria's Hindi is rusty from lack of use, so Nani translates the villagers' small talk. One of the famous trackers involved in the hunt is rumored to be involved in illicit smuggling activities. Tigers are said to never attack front-on, so hunters are running around with masks at the back of their heads, looking like Agni, the two-headed fire god. The dense forest is proving unnavigable for 4x4s, so elephants are being called in. There have been no recent sightings, but a neighbor's cousin said a horse was mauled a village over. Murmurs at this news betray a mixture of fear and awe, and no doubt as to the responsible party.

Ria has never been to her grandmother's village. It's been five years since she's seen Nani in person, back when her grandmother was still willing and able to stand the journey to New York City. But they video chat once a week, and Ria feels closer to Nani than her parents. Perhaps the level of generational remove allows her grandmother to show a bit more leniency as to Ria's life choices, which reflect scattered impulse rather than pursuit of any plan. Nani listens rather than lectures, tells Ria she is young and there's still the rest of her life to be tied to the long-schooled and well-paid professional paths her parents are pushing.

Over the last year, though, Ria had started to wonder whether she should be living a more settled life. She learned nearly every day of a friend's promotion, engagement, or pregnancy. Meanwhile, she'd been performing the motions of existence while waiting to discover something that truly moved her. Though her job title—"perfumer's apprentice"—inspired intrigued glances at parties or on dates, she had to shift the subject quickly. Any further conversation would reveal she was nothing more than a retail assistant in a dead-end position.

She'd gotten the job on pure whim, having gone to see the perfumer mostly to satisfy her curiosity, but also because he became—seemingly overnight—an unavoidable presence in her life. Every other post on her social media feeds was a paragraphs-long rave by an acquaintance about his products, and the mere thought of clicking on one of his ads resulted in his name shadowing her all over the internet. As she checked out her frozen curry and microwaveable rice at Trader Joe's, his tanned, thickly-bearded face stared at her from a holistic living magazine cover, mouth poised disdainfully as if about to say, *not homemade?*

His Williamsburg storefront had looked exactly as she'd expected it to, intimidatingly sparse with shelves of unpolished wood displaying glass vials like museum-quality artifacts. He'd been finishing up with another customer when she walked in, a woman in a yellow sundress who was fawning over how exquisitely he'd captured Cartagena. After the woman had left, the perfumer had turned to Ria and asked the place she wanted bottled. She'd written the name of her grandmother's village on a narrow sliver of a label, and he'd disappeared with this into a back room.

Ten minutes later, he'd emerged holding a slim glass vial with Ria's label stuck to it. Test it, he'd said, spraying a fine mist onto the patch of skin she offered him. Her wrist emanated humid fog and woodsmoke laced with leather, lemons, and honey. She had no way of knowing for sure, but to her, the scent seemed perfect. She could see how the perfumer had become so popular with a certain class of immigrants and their children. He charged more than any designer or celebrity for a comparable item, but still less than a plane ticket across several oceans.

Ria had been seduced by what the perfumer was selling: a salve for anyone homesick for an inherited place or desperate for a whiff of a memory. Moreover, she remembered that Nani had once mentioned she came from a long and ancient perfume tradition on that side of the family. Ria had asked for a job application and the perfumer had seemed startled; there was no sign anywhere indicating an available opening. But his expression had shifted quickly; she watched as he both contemplated and became attached to the idea of having an eager assistant, all in a matter of seconds. Ria was hired on the spot. She remembered having been excited to tell her grandmother about the new position, but also to quit scrounging for temp jobs, each one more mind-numbing than the last.

The perfumer's charm faded as quickly as the scents he bottled. Ria spent most of her days stocking boxes and mixing fragrances in the dingy, windowless backroom. There were wall-to-wall metal shelves filled with glass bottles surrounding a wobbly wooden table. Most of the bottles were carefully organized essences of an ordinary variety, none of the obscure treasures Ria had envisioned, like frankincense and ambergris and oudh.

One whole shelving unit was devoted to unlabeled square bottles, uniform in size and each filled with clear liquid. The perfumer instructed her to use this liquid as the base for any scent they prepared, to which they added a drop or two of a randomly selected essence. Ria assumed the liquid was some sort of alcohol solution, though it had a decidedly nonsterile and appealing scent.

At the end of her first week, she came across a cardboard box in the back alley by the dumpsters that contained the same bottles, only these ones still had intact labels. Each label said Chanel No. 5. Her own mother wore this perfume, collected bottles any times she found herself early for a flight with time to shop in airport duty-free. Ria was too ashamed she'd been fooled by the perfumer to confront him, and knew that exposing him would leave her jobless, again. As she considered her options, she also weighed heavily the fact that the back room was quiet, no office drama or water cooler banalities to endure. She didn't have to face a computer screen all day or fiddle with temperamental spreadsheets. She could work with her hands and occasionally hear shouts of joy from the front room as a customer recognized a familiar smell, already primed to connect it to their memories.

Luckily, Ria had had some money set aside. Ostensibly the funds were for grad school, the savings account a means of showing enough interest to stem the tide of her parents' badgering. But Nani had never asked Ria to visit before, not in so many words. Given her disillusionment—and the alternative that now presented itself—Ria had needed little additional inducement to leave her job at the perfumer's. On the morning she'd gone in to quit, the perfumer had tried to hand her a stack of bills, attempting to buy her silence. He had looked so pathetic in that moment, stripped of his usual mystical sheen. She'd refused the money, though, and offered to keep his secret anyway. She didn't see the point in revealing it; it would be like telling happier people they were taking a placebo, when that word itself meant *I will please.*

So she'd booked a flight that left as soon as possible. The context her grandmother provided was bare-bones, though still more information than Ria had known about her grandmother. She'd never realized how little Nani talked about herself. Nani, it turned out, lived in a tiger corridor that was plagued by a man-eating tigress. Eleven people had been allegedly killed by the beast over the past two years. A recent court ruling had given the necessary authorization to shoot to kill despite the tiger's endangered status. But pushback from environmental activists required an effort to at least try to trap the tigress first.

Nani—well-known and well-respected in the region for her fragrance-making expertise—had been asked to craft a scent to attract the tigress. Initially, she'd refused, citing the tremor in her right hand that had caused her to stop working years back. But then she'd thought of her granddaughter, who worked in a perfume store and might be eager to assist. She'd thought also of capitalizing on Ria's nascent interest in fragrance, there being so much knowledge she had still to share.

The next afternoon, having slept off her jet lag, Ria repurposes Nani's dining table into a workstation. She lays out a vinyl tablecloth, a few clean and empty glass jars, and a pile of toothpicks. She asks Nani where the essences are stored, finding no rows of neatly labeled bottles anywhere in the flat, aside from the spices in the kitchen. Nani bursts into laughter. Is this what he taught you? she says.

This surgical setup? My god. She laughs for several more minutes, but when she stops to catch her breath, her face looks rueful.

She leads Ria out the screen door in the kitchen to the backyard, still damp from the morning's rain. The small garden is untamed, like it's been left to its own devices for some time. A jasmine bush has eaten a stone wall, creeping up and over into a neighbor's property. Fruit trees have dropped once-ripe offerings on the ground to brown and fester. Nani points to a corner near a patch of determined marigolds, where a copper pot with a pipe extending from its lid squats on top of a pile of bricks. Here is where we work, she says.

Ria carries over a plastic chair and settles Nani in it a foot away. Following her grandmother's precise instructions, she gets a fire going in the brick structure's opening. In the copper pot above, she pours water and tosses in rose petals from the bush behind her. The bamboo pipe sends the fragrant steam to a shallow rectangular well she fills with oil. After a few hours, the smell is unmistakable, as clear as the fresh roses blooming behind her, with not a single false, chemical note. Her grandmother dips a finger into the oil and touches it gently to Ria's wrists and then her own.

She can tell Nani is beginning to tire, afternoon humidity turning the day languid and heavy. Ria takes

her in for a nap, holding Nani at the elbow to keep her
steady. Then she returns outside until it becomes too dark
to see what she's doing. There are so many combinations
she wants to test—a sliver of bark shaved from a camphor
tree, handfuls of cloves and fennel seeds. She scrubs her
wrists between each application until patches are red and
raw. Each time the oil meets her clean skin, it produces a
different smell entirely.

The hunt team returns by the weekend without a body.
The men look exhausted, faces covered in unruly beard
growth and dark circles beneath their eyes. As there's no
guesthouse or hotel close by, they split up to board with
a few families in town. One of the forest rangers stops
by Nani's house to nudge her for the scent, which they
are eager to slather on the traps. He says they will wait to
leave again until she's got one ready, but that had certainly
better be soon. She's had cubs now, the ranger adds. Soon
they'll be craving more than milk.

Ria doesn't have a sense yet of Nani's opinions about
the tigress. She has mixed feelings, herself, about the situation. She wonders if the tigress is sick of needing to
hide, of running into cement instead of a soft stand of
bushes, a belching factory where a tree with low branches
should be. Whether she had the cubs as a last-ditch effort

at continuing to exist, in the face of all the forces aimed at her demise.

Despite her reflexive sympathy for the hunted, Ria knows she is an outsider in the region. She understands nothing of the last several years' terror, all the villagers who are also simply trying to live on the same stretch of land. Some neighbors say the tigress has developed a bloodlust, while others say she kills humans because she has no choice.

How to catch a tiger, according to the nightly village gossip: Sharpshooters. Sniper rifles. Tranquilizer darts. Buffalo meat. Calvin Klein cologne. Solar lamps. Thermal imagery. At least six trained elephants. A trio of veterinarians. Zookeepers. Mahouts. That celebrity hunter guy, the one with the mustache. Bulldozers. Traps. Night-vision goggles. Drones. Army tanks. Cajoling. Pleading. Prayers. Smoke first. Then fire.

Nani chooses a scent based on musk, and Ria helps her tinker with quantities and notes. They are using plant proxies rather than deer glands, knowing that all the animal products put out for the tigress have already proved an insufficient lure. They are hoping to arouse her curiosity with a heady combination of mallow, okra, and hibiscus. Ria knows they're on the right track because the scent hits her nostrils like a punch in the face. The nearby gulmohar tree drops all of its blossoms, sickened by the stench. They bottle a few versions of the oil, which Ria packs into an airtight container. Nani calls the forest ranger staying a few doors down to come pick up the batches in the morning.

That night Ria crawls into bed with an unfamiliar feeling of accomplishment. Through the thin wall she can hear Nani's light snoring, a sound endearing only when made by her grandmother. A line of glass bottles glints on the dresser, catching the faint moonlight filtering through the curtains. During her grandmother's naps each afternoon, just before their evening walks to the edge of the forest, Ria has managed to concoct a few scents of her own. She has half a mind to set up a website when she goes back to New York so that she can sell them.

Sometime in the night, Ria wakes to a dull, gong-like sound. She lies still, staring at the ceiling, waiting for the noise to repeat. It doesn't, not after several minutes. Ria pulls on a dressing gown and tiptoes to the screen door in the back. The sound—if it wasn't a dream remnant—seemed to have come from the backyard. She thinks she'll just take a look outside to be sure a monkey or some other mischievous animal has not been tempted by the fallen fruits in the garden.

The moon is a barely visible crescent, and half covered by a cloud. There is no other light source in the backyard. In the darkness Ria's eyes make out orange in the corner by the copper pot, but her brain tells her it is only the marigolds. On her second scan of the yard, she glimpses ears and stripes in the orange, though it takes several more moments to comprehend what she is looking at. As their eyes meet, the tigress remains perfectly motionless, seemingly nonplussed at being seen. She sits calmly on her haunches with an erect, regal posture. It is Ria who blinks first. She pivots slowly and runs to Nani's bedroom, clutching the landline phone.

The tigress is still in the backyard when the forest ranger arrives. He brings with him a hunter who is carrying a rifle upright against his side, butt in palm and barrel against shoulder. The men stand by the screen door, surveying the backyard for several minutes. Look at her, they whisper. At last, at last we meet. The ranger and the hunter debate a plan of action. They don't want to open the door for fear of startling the tigress back into the woods. They could send someone around to the other side of the garden wall to set a trap, but there's no guarantee, given her intelligence and stealthiness, that she'll run into it.

Ria stops listening to the men's bickering. She watches the tigress, who has managed to get the top of the pot open by batting the lid with her enormous front paws. Ria had cleaned it carefully after each use, but traces of the scent must have remained. Perhaps she'd grown too accustomed to the smells to even register them anymore. The tigress sniffs deeply at the pot and the oil well a few times, her eyes closed. She stretches luxuriously, showing off a body that seems boneless, as if it is made only of seamless, powerful muscle. Then she begins rolling around on the ground with what looks, to Ria's human eyes, like pleasure.

From the dining table behind her, she hears Nani clear her throat. Ria looks at the men. She sees they are using a switchblade to slowly cut a circle out of the screen door, which looks like it will just accommodate the tip of the rifle the hunter is now wielding, barrel out, from his shoulder. The tigress is still on her back, scratching herself against tree roots and dirt, her head facing up to the moon. Ria turns and catches her grandmother's eye, telegraphs a desire without speaking.

Nani calls the men over, and though they try at first to brush her off, they cannot ignore the request of an elder in her own home. They place the rifle and switchblade on the floor carefully and go crouch next to Nani's chair. The three of them whisper together for several minutes, after which the two men stand, the hunter looking angry and the ranger looking resigned. From the front door, the ranger retrieves a gun with an extra-long, extremely slender barrel. He loads in a dart with a pink-feathered tail and kneels on the ground by the hole in the screen they've fashioned. After a few darts, the tigress's eyes close and she goes still.

The men hurry into the backyard for a closer look. In the ensuing silence, Ria asks her grandmother what she'd said to convince them to tranquilize instead of kill. They are unmarried and childless, Nani says. I told them it was bad luck to kill a tiger in a widow's home, that they would be cursed to never have children as a result. I don't think they really believed me, but I suppose it wasn't a risk they were willing to take.

Ria retreats to her bedroom when the rest of the hunt team descends on the house for removal. She isn't interested in watching. But the men carry the limp tigress around to the front, load the stretcher onto a flatbed truck idling several yards ahead on the road. The whole loud procession is clearly visible from the window facing her bed, difficult to sleep through, more so to turn away from.

⁂

A few months later, Ria learns that the tigress has died. An article reports that she passed of unknown causes at the Delhi Zoo. Her cubs had been trapped soon after her, and all three were sent to live together in a revamped tiger exhibit. There had been a small parade in the village streets following the capture, the hunt team riding elephants and waving from open-topped jeeps. Activists who had been ready to protest applauded, instead, the humane captures using musk oil. The village returned quickly to a place of the living, the collective sense of relief palpable. Before Ria left, a construction crew broke ground on a logging plant at the trailhead where she and Nani walked each evening.

Since returning to New York City, Ria has rented a minuscule live/work studio in outer Queens, in which she's fashioned a makeshift stovetop still. But she misses the open fire method of Nani's backyard, scents already airborne and mingling from the forest and flowers around her. During their regular calls, Ria sees that Nani is now ailing more noticeably. She can't hold the phone for longer than a few minutes and has trouble remembering things, takes a beat longer than normal to place events or people in context. When Ria mentions the tigress's death, Nani first says, who? Then she says hunters keep asking her for musk oil, but she tells them she's forgotten how to make it. Ria catches a fleeting twinkle in Nani's eyes that may or may not be the pixel-blur of a poor connection.

After she hangs up, Ria checks for Delhi Zoo videos, which she does at least once a week. She finds a new one of the tiger enclosure, a short clip of the cubs. They look nearly full-grown now. She had expected them to be pacing, as many big cats do in zoos. But the cubs are sitting on their haunches next to each other, with the same erect posture their mother had. They gaze expectantly at the person holding the camera. As if, Ria thinks, they are waiting for a piece of vital information to be imparted— for some creature to tell them how to survive in the world, or at least how to live in captivity.

Pillow Book of the Dead
Prince's Intended

Yesterday marked eleven years within these walls, which are still bare except for an extended series of patiently scrawled tally clusters. A palace attendant slipped a special meal through the slot in the bungalow's locked front door while I was sleeping. They are careful that I never see the errand boy or girl's face—or even glimpse a hand—but the groceries trickle in like clockwork each week to supplement the twelve years' worth of provisions that were left in the storeroom.

If anything ever happens to their palace chef, I will know within a year because he always cooks the same meal for this day: turmeric rice with stuffed baby eggplants, accompanied by a sweet yogurt lassi.

I warmed the meal in the kitchen and ate while standing, seeing as there was no one around to tut-tut this grossly informal behavior. After washing and drying my steel plate, I went to the dead prince's room and washed and dried his body. I pushed his thick black hair off his forehead and lit a stick of puja-grade incense in the corner. *Happy anniversary, dear*, I told him before gently closing the door behind me.

THINGS I SHOULD HAVE LISTENED TO MORE CLOSELY

- The palace seer when he prophesied, all through my youth, *you will marry a dead man*
- Nearby chattering crows, whose gossip appears to rival that of my most conversationally skilled lady-in-waiting
- My father, the king, when I overheard him say, *a king who has borne only a single daughter is in a desperate position indeed*
- The palace crier, who must have delivered the news of the mysterious illness and sudden death of the neighboring kingdom's only prince—but not his burial or funeral rites—while I was absent or not listening

- How even the most vibrant peacock's call sounds uncannily like a woman screaming
- On the eve of my sixteenth birthday, the celebratory song played by the court sitar player and commissioned specially for the occasion, which began with the requisite pomp and circumstance but drifted like a meandering river farther and farther from its beginning until it ended with nothing more than one note plucked and quickly dampened

Every morning, the dawn filters through the single sitting room window and delivers a matching rectangle on the tiled floor. The shape is slightly slanted, a bit fuzzed around the edges. I see myself in this duplicate shape; I have grown less clear about my contours the longer I stay here. The patch is warm to the touch, though not as warm as a pane of glass heated by the sunrise, and even less warm than an inch of my skin. There is never enough warmth to go around.

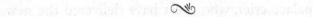

THINGS I WILL NEVER EAT AGAIN ONCE I LEAVE HERE

- Turmeric rice
- Stuffed baby eggplants

- Sweet lassi
- My heart out
- My words

❧

I have been having a recurring dream of the bungalow, though I have not seen its exterior since I entered it over a decade ago.

I first came across the bungalow on a royal leisure trip, one insisted upon by the queen. She had noticed—in the preternatural way of mothers—that quotidian palace life had been reduced for me to a dull monotony. My malaise rose to an actionable issue when it began manifesting in my interactions with the very short line of suitors that had started to come calling.

Facing frothed waves on one side and snowcapped peaks on the other, our kingdom was renowned for its beauty but also isolated enough that few, if any, visitors arrived by chance and even fewer on purpose. I knew my parents had gone to great lengths to solicit potential mates for me, but I could not muster even a fraction of the charm that had been trained into my body from birth. When I was asked to sing, I forgot lyrics and could not stay on key; when I was asked to dance, I pitched out of the steps and tripped over my own feet; when I was asked to serve our guests, I developed a violent stomachache and retreated with mumbled apologies to my chambers.

The tenor of my parents' discussions grew frantic, and it was decided that we would decamp for a time to the woods of the mountainous neighboring kingdom. It was assumed that the crisp, unsalted air and the opportunity for quiet contemplation would right my wandering mind and soothe my anxious body.

OCCASIONS WHEN TIME DRAGS BY

- The moment just before a dawning realization but after it is too late to do anything differently based on the coming epiphany
- Twelve years—even when you know, going in, that it will be twelve years
- Small-talk with a suitor once it is obvious he has never, in his life, spoken to anyone about a topic other than himself
- Announcements from the palace crier during wedding season and monsoon season, when it seems everyone is either sliding into love or sliding off of cliffs
- Waking in the middle of the night to the realization of one's own fate, as if the information has just been learned anew and you must do the long and difficult work of accepting it once again

A week into the leisure trip it became obvious that the outing was merely a smaller-scale simulacrum of palace life. The trip came complete with lavish meals, the usual coterie of attendants and hangers-on, and an openness to our days that somehow devoured the will to do anything but idly stroke the tassels of a silk pillow and watch the breeze dislodge the pointed leaves of an overgrown neem tree.

One afternoon I begged to be released from the royal gathering, claiming uncontrollable nausea. My parents had grown superstitious about my bouts of fragility and ordered the attendants to heed my demand for privacy. I retreated to my personal tent, which had been stuffed with objects that looked marooned in the cavernous area, such as wool carpets, leather poufs, and side tables adjacent only to empty space.

A bowl of pomegranate seeds had been left out in a silver bowl, the pips glittering like a palmful of rubies. I reached over to pluck one from the heap but the movement of my hand sparked the droning of a fly, which took off toward me in a flash of pearlescent wings. I called out several times for someone to fetch a swatter before realizing that I had requested all of my attendants to stay away. In other words, I had asked for and received exactly this desired moment of solitude. Why, then, did I feel so incapable of accepting and enjoying it?

CARE-TAKING INSTRUCTIONS FOR THE DEAD PRINCE

- Fluff pillow beneath his head, twice daily
- With warm water and a soft cloth, wash and dry his body, daily
- With warm water and a sharp-edged blade, shave his chin and cheeks, daily
- Massage his skin with soothing aromatic oils, daily
- Clothe his body in freshly washed linen trousers and silk tunic, daily
- Perform a puja to bless his soul and dormant life-force and enable its safe return, daily
- Recite one hour of devotional poetry to him, daily
- Clip his fingernails and toenails, weekly
- Clip the edges of his mustache, weekly
- Clip his hair, weekly
- Perform an anniversary puja to bless his soul and dormant life-force and enable its safe return, yearly
- Feed him the elixir-to-be-provided that will wake him, duodecennially

A group of muscular attendants accompanying the leisure trip had erected my tent on a ridge overlooking a field of wild poppies and bellflowers. The colors swirled below like the border pattern of a finely-woven carpet. I had been surrounded by fresh flowers my entire life—jasmine for my hair, marigolds for my pujas, lotus for my ponds, hibiscus for the pleasure of my eyes—but had never once walked among buds still rooted in the soil. I was gripped by a sudden wish to stroll through the high-altitude meadow, to let the scents mingle together in my nostrils. Along the way I idly collected a bouquet of flowers, which I wrapped in a piece of gold string I pulled off the fringe of my sari's pallu.

At the edge of the field, a crowd of tall and thin evergreen trees stood watch. The air cooled considerably once I crossed back into the forest. I relished the sensation of shivering, the way my body spasmed to reject the lack of its accustomed-to levels of comfort. There was no path, so I simply walked and walked until the soles of my feet began bleeding, and then I continued walking. I had the vague sensation that I was ascending the mountain, but the woods blocked any view of my position. I noticed after a time that I was walking not on a bed of pine needles but on a fresh coat of snow. My red footprints—stark against the untouched white—looked like those of a blood-lusting rakshasi or else those of a struggling human in grave danger.

Some hours passed and I sensed a deeper darkness within the forest. I guessed that the sun had set and began to panic at having followed my own foolish impulses to an unfamiliar, far-flung patch of woods. I sat on a fallen tree trunk, which was decomposing at its roots end into a miniature forest of wide-capped mushrooms. I wondered whether my extended absence had set off alarm bells back at the royal campsite. How long would it be before anyone sent to search might actually find me? Lost in this miserable reverie, I almost missed the beckoning flash of white in the forest ahead.

MORE TRAPPED THAN I

- All the princesses and goddesses in their titular constellations
- The still-beating heart in its close-walled ribcage
- A tiger crouched in dense underbrush, once sighted by the hunter's rifle
- Thunder, which must always unroll dully and ostentatiously after the quick and dazzling lightning
- A thousand years into the cycle of rebirth, still atoning for a sin you never witnessed
- Women of any social position other than (if I'm honest) my own

That recurring dream I am having: hidden behind an especially dense grouping of trees, I find a small bungalow in such immaculate condition that I assume it must be inhabited. Only when the right current of wind shifts a high-up tree branch does the moonlight reach the dwelling, bouncing off the whitewashed exterior and producing the momentary shine that catches my eye. The wooden door, too, is painted white, though there is a message scrawled in a vivid red that looks to have been mixed from kumkum powder. I read the message as if it is meant for me. There is no one else around for at least fifty thousand paces. It says: *Here lies our kingdom's beloved dead prince, who will wake in twelve years on X-X-XXXX. This door will open only for a dutiful woman carrying an offering that the gods favor: this woman shall be the dead prince's bride.* I am carrying my wildflower bouquet in one hand; with the other, I reach toward the golden doorknob. When I touch it, it easily turns.

THINGS IT IS FRUSTRATING OR EMBARRASSING TO WITNESS

- One's own mortality / one's own fate
- A proud man who has resolved to kneel for no one, bowing to my father

- Court musicians ceasing play midsong to tune their instruments
- A beautifully ripe custard apple, which, when split open, reveals the green fuzz of mold metastasizing on its insides
- Someone who is winning a game of parcheesi until an opponent lands on their space and sends them back to the start
- Desperation
- A messenger who has arrived after great expense and fanfare and then forgets the message he had been forced to memorize
- A prone man's naked, impotent body

It occurs to me that one might wonder whether—after all this time—I love the dead prince.

Do I love him?

I am currently devoted to him. Is that the same thing?

THINGS I KNOW ABOUT THE DEAD PRINCE

- From X Kingdom
- The names of his parents
- That he is an only child

- That he is the subject of very fervent prophecies about reanimation
- Well-fed in life
- Average to below-average size for a male of my kingdom
- Locations of every birthmark
- That he has a scar in his mustache from which the hair grows slightly askew
- That if I press open his eyelids, I see the reflection of my own face in his pupils

The dead prince heard my life story today. It was the hundredth time I told it, all the way through from my birth to my slow death at his unmoving hands. A few years ago I took to elaborating on the story, so that it now includes an imagined passage involving my parents. *They looked for days*, I tell him, *but never found me. Only when they beseeched the neighboring kingdom for help did they learn what had transpired. A lavish engagement party was held in our absence, widely attended by the citizens and royal families of both kingdoms. The kings rejoiced at the power of their joined kingdoms, the trade that flourished with increased cooperation and amity. It's for the best, my father told my mother. Or else, he said: there was no other way.*

I leave the door to the dead prince's room open while I tell my story, shouting so I can be sure my voice can still attain a certain volume, if and when the time comes. For exercise I walk through the rooms while speaking. The circuit includes the sitting room, the kitchen, the store-room, the dead prince's room, and my room.

My room is my favorite one in the bungalow. The walls are the lightest yellow, a color so slight I wonder if it is merely the paint showing signs of age. There is a large daybed beneath the window that has bolster pillows and a thick brocade spread. I moved the bookshelves over from the sitting room, and whatever time I do not spend cooking or caretaking, I spend here. I was left only devotional poetry and several religious texts, but of late I have taken to writing my own words between the lines. On the end pages I sketched a view of the distant mountain, which in the right dusk-light looks like the sloped fin of a barra-mundi, as apt to suddenly flit away and be lost to the dark, sweeping tide.

THINGS THAT ARE BITTERSWEET

- The mournful shehnai accompanying the bride's entry at a wedding
- A sitting room when you have no visitors

- New moon nights
- The marriage of your closest and only friend
- A tree that has lost its leaves to the season
- Familial love
- Memories of a life you no longer live
- A completely empty shoreline
- Anniversaries

I have been expecting no one so long I imagine my own heartbeat is the sound of approaching footsteps.

THINGS THAT MAKE THE HEART BEAT FAST

- The face of one's beloved (I imagine)
- Disobeying one's parents
- Offering one's opinion in a room crowded with elders
- Banging one's fists on a locked door for hours
- A fractured and fleeting glimpse of sunrise after months of dense, stubborn foliage that will not yield to the stunning view
- A milestone you never imagined reaching, suddenly fast approaching

❧

I was not sure how the life-giving elixir would present itself, but when I went to retrieve the twelfth anniversary meal from the front door, I glimpsed a sliver of unnatural green through the slim gap between the slot and the floor. From the sitting room window, I saw that there was a woman in a faded emerald-colored sari sitting cross-legged on the ground in front of the bungalow. I pounded on the glass of the window until I got her attention. She looked over at me and smiled. Her face seemed vaguely familiar though I was certain I had never seen her in our palace court before. She was dressed like an attendant, simply adorned with her pallu tucked protectively around her waist.

She held up a glass bottle filled with a milky-looking liquid and then pointed at the message on the door. I understood this to mean she did not possess the power to open it. *I'll push this through the slot,* she said. *I just wanted to make sure you got it. My king will be arriving shortly, as will a priest who will perform your marriage.*

I nodded, and she passed out of my line of sight as she approached the door. I stood on the other side, feeling electrified by the presence, after so long, of another living person. I listened to her steady breathing, its full, wave-like sound. I heard her hand touch the doorknob, which was an impulse I understood; I myself had been unable to resist. Then I saw the knob turn, and the door open, and then the woman stood there, gaping at me, so shocked she nearly dropped the bottle.

THINGS THE CROWS SAID IN THEIR DAILY PARLEYS

- Caw caw caw
- Crraaaa-aaaa
- Raaahhhhhh
- Akraw akraw
- Fly-flyyy-fleeeeee

What offering was it that the gods had favored? Not my bouquet or her bottle but merely the fact of our bodies, any body? I shuddered to think that the front door might have been locked, all this time, only from the inside; that a prophecy could operate not by predestination but instead the vagaries of cold, hard chance.

Having lacked human contact for so long, I will admit my reflexes were sluggish. I was still trying to clear the low fog within my brain when the attendant pushed past me, running from room to room until she located the dead prince.

I followed her to the back of the bungalow, where I came upon her prying open the dead prince's mouth. *Drink*, she said, *drink*, as she poured the elixir down his throat. I didn't move to stop her. Her formerly placid features were now scrunched together from the effort of keeping the dead prince's jaws open. I recognized that she wanted him in a proactive, impassioned way; as a means of changing her fate, rather than—as for me—becoming settled to it.

A moment passed in which she was studying the urn-shaped birthmark on the dead prince's left wrist and did not notice that he had opened his eyes. I watched as he blinked and focused on her face—which was really quite lovely—hovering above his own. I suppose I was meant, then, to imagine myself in the attendant's place, to begrudge her this first glance. But I felt only dread dissipating from my body, the beginnings of weightlessness. My shoulders lifted of their own accord and straightened.

Beloved, the prince croaked at the attendant. *My bride*. After tentatively wriggling his fingers a few times, he took her ringless hand. The smile that gradually subsumed his features was beatific, one that might have stirred a heart that was the right sort of willing. Then he stood, gingerly, and began making a small lap around the room to shake out the sleep from his legs. The attendant looked nervously to the doorway where I was standing;

she was clearly expecting some sort of reckoning for her sudden usurpation. I let the prince shuffle along until he came to me.

And who are you? the prince whispered, not yet capable of full voice. Meeting his gaze, I felt a slight pang of attachment to him, the kind bred by extended proximity. Like love for longstanding fixtures or furniture whose provenance now escapes you—objects that seem integral to your existence until finally given up or away. I suspected that any allegiance forged by force of circumstance could be swiftly overcome, provided a certain degree of time and space.

I'm no one, I said. *I merely brought the life-giving elixir.* I bowed and backed out of the room. Between the attendant and me, I couldn't say which of our faces looked more can't-believe-my-luck at my exit. In the sitting room I found the untouched anniversary meal coated by a swarm of black flies. I continued outside, letting the breeze caress my wind-starved face, eavesdropping on the trees' intimate whisperings. I took the soft path into and out of the woods, toward the diamond-sun studding the horizon, away and farther away from the bungalow, where I'd left the front door hanging wide open, an answer for anyone who might later ask why I'd left and where I'd gone.

Marigolds

THE BLUFF

You live on a bluff just before the edge of the world, facing the sea. Where there would be dragons, according to ancient illustrated maps, though you have never spotted such a creature. Once, when you were 9, you were shivering before the drop after a spent storm, watching the heaving water subside into its usual rhythms. The clouds clustered around the sun like moths trying to suffocate a flame. Yet one weak beam eventually slipped through, illuminating a swirl of eddies. Beneath which: shimmering, undulating scales. Did you glimpse: (I) one mythic being or (II) dozens of ordinary ones, moving collectively? You tell yourself the latter. But for a moment it had seemed possible to fool yourself—to inhabit, however briefly, another world that had been layered onto yours.

The house you live in is too close to the sea. Horizontally, not vertically; it is precipitously perched like an aerie, nestled in the gray sky. You feel vertigo sometimes looking through the back wall of windows. The panes are thick, reinforced glass but still seem fragile when compared to the elements or the black crags of rock below. You have felt on the verge for years.

Whoever built this house had hubris; whoever built it must have scorned humans as much as it seems your mother does, because the nearest neighbor is a mile away. The closest town is ten miles farther, infrequently visited for stock-up trips in an old Peugeot hatchback that otherwise rusts in the driveway. This seems to suit your mother perfectly. She has been retreating so slowly you'd barely noticed, a butterfly cocooning to metamorphose back to a caterpillar. The cocoon is the house. The cocoon is each room within it, filled with hundreds of books from which she schooled you herself. Your schooling is now done; she has taught you what she wished. You do not think the cocoon has room for you. She thinks you are ready to fly.

Entire days can now pass with no words exchanged between you, the two of you alive and alone at the edge of the world. Each of you in your worlds. The worlds drawn around you tight. Your mother spends her days with other voices in her head, one-sided conversations that do not demand any response from her. She works as a transcriptionist, faithfully documenting dictations sent to her from authors, lawyers, and corporate executives. The hallways echo with the clickety-clack of her typing. When she gets caught up in a task and forgets to eat, you bring her a plate of fruit, a bowl of soup, a toasted sandwich. Thank you, she mouths, gratitude apparent on her face, but she doesn't remove her headphones.

So yes, you crave the company of others. For sounds beyond the drafts whistling and howling through the house, its foundations audibly sinking and creaking beneath you. For a house made of something other than wind, which carries nothing you can hold.

You have lived here as long as you can remember, which is not to say your whole life. No one remembers their whole life. It seems unjust that early childhood, ostensibly one's happiest years, is largely unrememberable. What has your mother told you about your life? What is it that you know but do not remember? (I) You emerged, squalling, in a county hospital an hour away and you haven't been farther since. (II) You roamed nearly feral through this landscape for years, a new queen for a forgotten realm. Do the gulls and badgers and hares now recognize your crownless head? (III) You almost drowned twice, the water mercifully spitting you back up on the rocks each time. You, the scraped-up, would-be mermaid.

But there is much that is outside the reach of your memory. Much that is not recollected to you. Your mother has said she is shielding you from things she wishes she did not remember. You have the sense that the past is a storm she is trying to outrun. She is trying to hide in a place that was scarcely imaginable to her before she arrived. She crossed an ocean thinking, ahead: blank slate. Clear skies. Or: a storm of my own choosing.

You, though, would not have chosen these bonedrench rains and gutpunch winds and the ceaseless cloud cover. You want nothing more than to leave the sea's brink. To mirror your mother's journey: go as far as possible, arrive at another edge of the world. But you cannot leave, or you cannot bring yourself to. Leaving means leaving your mother alone with the storm. If you were not there, you think she would let it swallow her.

What do you do with your days, then? You often walk to the trail that begins a couple miles down the coast and proceeds several miles farther to a historic lighthouse. In pleasant weather there are sometimes people out for the day, walking solo or in pairs or with dogs. This area of the country is renowned for its beauty. If you had not lived here as long as your memory, you think you could find it beautiful. You like to stand at the trailhead, by the crumbling stone wall that runs alongside, and rub a patch of furry lichen like a rabbit's foot for luck. You are wishing for someone to talk to.

Today, two women walk by you at the trailhead within minutes of each other.

(I) One woman is carrying a hard hat and wearing a half-zip sweatshirt with a lighthouse embroidered on the front.

(II) The other is carrying a hard black case and wearing a button-down shirt and khaki vest with numerous pockets.

Whom should you speak to?

I. Lighthouse woman is tall and walks with purpose but slows upon noticing you scurrying to match her long strides. Hello, you say, beautiful weather we're having. This opening is always effective; it is like the sun is the mutual acquaintance of everyone here and mention of her shining face is an instant form of connection.

Yes, the woman says, glancing at her phone. She seems a bit distracted. Hope it holds. We're scheduled to start work in two weeks and can't really afford to get rain delayed.

Right, you say. Fingers crossed, though around now we usually do see a turn. What are you working on?

The woman points to the lighthouse on her sweatshirt. I'm part of the project shifting Eddysedge inland.

Before it falls into the sea, you know? Not a whole lot of ships trying to come in round here, but it's one of the oldest on this stretch of coastline, so it seemed worth saving.

You, living in your house at the edge of the world, are familiar with erosion, a fatal disease eating away at the coastline. The waves devouring beaches, hollowing out the chalk cliffs. When you were a child, your mother would take you down to the beach by the lighthouse and stand at the far edge of the sand while you ran from her forward into the waves. You wondered why she chose to stand so far from you. Her tiny figure, silhouetted by the lighthouse rising up behind, striped red and white like the barbershop pole in town. Looking back from the water, that distance across the sand seemed uncrossable. Now, that distance is nonexistent.

Yes, you say, the sea is getting awful close. I'd heard about this project. Glad it's moving along.

Is glad the right word, though? You aren't quite sure. The lighthouse is mostly nonfunctional, now just an ornament affixed to the landscape. You'd overheard the estimated cost for the project once in town and your jaw dropped. No one is coming to save you, your mother, and your house from the sea, not for any amount of money.

Ahead, the tip of the lighthouse has become visible. The trail will fork, the left side traveling down to the lighthouse and the right continuing to follow the coastline.

Hey, the woman says suddenly. Are you from around here?

You nod.

Odd question, but did someone recently pass away nearby? The other day I noticed what looked like maybe a shrine by the trail a few paces on. Orange flowers, a small pool of water. I'm up here most days of late and hadn't seen it before. Just wondering.

You are up here many days, too, and have never seen what the woman is talking about. You tell her no one around here has died recently, not that you know of. Not that you would know of much. But now you are wondering, too.

II. Many Pockets Woman is whistling under her breath, something that sounds animal rather than human. She startles when she notices you and seems to grip her black case more tightly. You are somewhat used to this reaction, knowing you and your mother's shade of brown is an unusual sight in this area.

Hello, you say. Beautiful weather we're having.

The woman visibly relaxes at this. Yes, she says, it's perfect. Best I've seen in the last couple weeks.

Indeed, you say. What brings you out here?

Well, she says, I'm an ornithologist. Specializing in sea birds. A few months ago I got a call saying someone had spotted a blue-bellied storm petrel nearby. That's a bird we'd thought extinct for years. So I had to come see if this was a hoax or an amateur misidentification or the real thing, which would be amazing.

Wow, you say. Does sound like an amazing find if it is real. Do you have a sense yet?

A feeling, she says. Real. The other day I was down by the rocks past the lighthouse and heard what I was certain was its call. I made sure to bring my recording equipment this time. Haven't seen the bird yet, though.

I hope you do soon, you say.

You aren't sure, though, if you do hope the bird is real. If it is, what if it's the last one of its kind? Would it know? You aren't sure what's sadder, the bird singing knowingly for only itself or unknowingly for only creatures that won't understand it. Better a hoax, you think. Let the dead birds lie.

You pass the lighthouse, noticing a flurry of activity around its base, trucks and construction equipment amassed down the trail. The woman says she'll have to turn off the trail soon to the rocky outcroppings where the bird has been known to roost.

Ironic, though, she says, after a short period of silence. If I do see the petrel, sailors' superstition says that we'll soon get bad weather. The birds are said to hold the souls of drowned sailors.

You give her a rueful smile. You have a healthy respect for superstition. It is an unknowable force like the sea, one it seems better not to cross.

Speaking of, the woman says, is this little altar thing up here for a lost sailor?

She motions to the left. Patches of yellow gorse coat much of the clifftops, so it's difficult at first to see what she's pointing at. Beneath one of the shrubs several paces away you see a small pool of water and a burst of orange flowers.

THE PORTAL

The shrubs fight you the whole way, actively resisting your advance. You arrive at last into a small clearing in the gorse. It is just a few steps from the cliff's edge. To your left you can see the lighthouse, and ahead to your right, below, you can just spot a person in a vest scrambling over the foaming rocks.

Below you is a pool of silvery water, round like a coin, about three feet across. A planted garland of orange flowers—marigolds, you think, which typically grow nowhere near here—rings the pool's periphery. You wonder for a moment if the flowers are fake and reach down to touch one. Its petals are plush, velvety, signaling the true thing. You cannot resist the urge to pluck the flower, the head popping off readily from the stem. You tuck it into the tail of your braided hair.

You regard the pool again, your own reflection, all the tendrils the wind has pulled out to frame your face. Not a shrine, you think, or an altar, though the arrangement of the components certainly suggests a human hand. The placement feels like an opening rather than a closure.

A gust of wind disturbs the surface of the pool. You jump back, expecting the water to slosh over onto your boots. But it doesn't; it slides to the edge and then continues upward, as if contained in an invisible cylinder. It drips vertically in a reverse waterfall until you are facing what looks like a full-size oval mirror. You glance around you, but there is no one in the vicinity to confirm what you are seeing.

Do you trust what you're seeing? (I) The stark landscape of your childhood has cultivated in you a healthy sense of wonder as to what nature is capable of, what it can reveal to you. (II) The stark landscape of your childhood has left you unsure of what humans are capable of revealing to you.

The wind leaves small ripples that invite you to touch. You reach for the water, cool like the sea. The opening beckons you closer. It hums like a low chant, an invitation.

You step forward and pass through.

The first thing you notice is the humidity. It weights the hot air pressing against you on all sides; at home, the air does not ever stop to caress you. You peel off your jacket.

You are standing on a beach facing another sea. It looks as endless as the one at home, but you know this is not your sea. How have you arrived here? Your stomach is fluttering, filled with a flock of birds trying to escape. The birds are fear. The birds are excitement. The place does not feel entirely unfamiliar. Do you know it? How could you, who have never left your corner of the earth, know it?

There are dozens of people around, people who look like you, people enjoying strolls with food from the circulating vendors or chasing running, laughing children or dipping their toes in the gently breaking waves. A boy near you is flying a yellow kite that hangs above in some invisible breeze. There is a lighthouse in the distance, sprouting from a stone platform in the harbor. You can just make out its stripes.

You can feel a great height looming behind you, but when you turn you see not cliffs but skyscrapers, the hulking buildings of a city, filled in all its corners with people. People, everywhere. You have never seen so many people. You are unsure how you are suddenly among so many people. But you are; you are here; you cannot leave so quickly.

You walk away from the sea toward the buildings and the sound of surf is replaced with the honking of vehicles cramming lanes and lanes of traffic. You hold your breath as you run across the road. At the corner across from you, a telephone pole leans beneath a jumble of black wires looped around its top like a cancerous growth. In the tangled nest you spot a flash of color. As you approach, two red-bellied birds emerge and fly away ahead. You feel the urge to follow.

(I) One bird is turning down the side street to your left.

(II) The other is headed down the one on your right.

Which way will you go?

I. You follow the bird left. This side street is no less crowded than the main road you've just turned off. You are awash in human smells: breathing, sweating, cooking, pissing. Animal smells, too. Hunger stirs within you. You cannot remember when you last ate, which makes you worry you are turning into your mother.

As if hearing your stomach's audible protests, the bird pauses its flight and perches on an awning above a sweet shop. Through the window you see tiers of multicolored delicacies displayed in a glass case. You have no names for any of these treats, budding in their trays like an edible garden—rows of pink and yellow doughy mounds, silver-coated rolls, nut-encrusted diamonds, glossy orange twisted strands.

The shop is tiny, with space enough to hold just the display case and room for one or two people to stand in front of it. As you enter, an elderly man reading a newspaper behind the case looks up. He meets your eyes with surprise.

Gita? Is that you?

You look behind you, reflexively, as you do when someone calls a name in your direction that isn't yours. There is no one else here but you. Gita is not your name, but it is your mother's.

No, you say, sorry.

The man looks confused. But—, he says, it is you . . . no?

You shake your head and he continues looking at you, his face still questioning. It is as if he is really asking, are you sure you're not her? And his face is kindly and so crestfallen you think maybe you could be. But he doesn't press you further.

There are a lot of people in this city, he says. I see a lot of faces. My mistake.

What do you recommend? you ask. Once the question is out of your mouth, you remember you don't have money on you to pay for anything.

Really anything, he says. This shop has been my family's for years. We make everything ourselves. His posture has shifted as he says this, his back a bit straighter, his chest a bit prouder.

It does all look wonderful, you say. But I'm sorry, I have to go now. I'll hopefully come back later.

Okay, the man says. No problem. But take this in the meantime.

He crouches over to reach into the glass case, reemerging with a caramel-colored slab dotted with seeds.

Chikki, he says. Gita's favorite, he adds, with a wink.

You thank the man and leave. Outside, the bird is waiting on the awning. You take a bite of the brittle and the shard dissolves sweet and salty in your mouth, a perfect mixture of tastes. The bird takes off and leads you farther into the maze of the city. Eventually, it lands on the head of a statue in front of a set of imposing Gothic buildings flanked by shade trees and palms. You think this must be a campus of some sort. While you are taking in the buildings, the bird flies somewhere out of your sight. You cross over into an open green space that lies, protected, behind the facades lining the road.

II. You follow the bird right. There are fewer people on this street. It looks more residential, towering apartment buildings affixed on top of car parks, all set behind walls with peeling paint. There are fewer shops on this street.

You walk straight for some time, listening to the low throb of the city and its punctuation, neighbors exclaiming between windows, motorcycles pausing, sputtering, before starting again, a passerby offering a lowball price, questioningly, to a vegetable seller. Eventually, the density of shops picks up again, and you notice the bird slowing, weaving back and forth above the street. It stops on the sign for a used bookstore. Through the smudged window you can see lines of narrow shelves, so tightly packed they seem to barely allow passage between them.

Bells above the door jingle as you enter. A man with glasses and a sweater vest emerges from the back of the shop, turning sideways to pass between two shelves.

Hello, he says, without looking at you. When he reaches the front of the shop he sees your face and smiles. Gita! Want to see what was just dropped off today?

You have never been mistaken for your mother before. The name feels jarring spoken aloud, because you have rare occasion to hear it.

No, you say, I'm not Gita, sorry. I would still love to see those books, though.

He is squinting at you through his glasses, not understanding your denial. He walks over to a stack of books piled next to the cash register on the counter. He hovers there protectively, considering you.

Okay, he says, I suppose that's fine. Someone just came in and donated these, so I haven't even had time to catalog them.

Not many people come in here, he adds. But Gita does, all the time. She's browsed through most of the shop now, so I like to tell her whenever anything's new.

He's still studying you, as if waiting for you to admit you're her. You almost want to, but you're you, so you can't.

That's very nice of you, you say. At this the man retreats again to the back of the store, leaving you to peruse the pile.

The stack is mostly tattered copies of novels and plays in English: Shakespeare, Dickens, Hardy. At the bottom there is an illustrated book of folklore, which you flip open. The binding is cracked, and the book settles automatically on two pages at the center. The picture on the right is of a friendly looking demon cradling a baby in one elbow and with the other hand placing an identical looking baby into a basket on the ground. You close the book.

Thank you, you call in the direction of the back of the shop.

Welcome, comes the reply. You leave and find the bird still nestled on the sign. It takes off and leads you down an endless succession of side streets. Eventually, you come to an imposing set of Gothic buildings with a statue of a man on a pedestal out front. The bird rests on the statue's head. Behind the buildings, you can just glimpse an open green space, a respite from the city's endless buildings. You cross the street to enter it.

THE CHANGELING

Here, in the green space behind the buildings, you find yourself still among so many people, mostly your age, toting books and backpacks and sitting in the grass. The stone buildings lining the space look warm and red in the afternoon light. At the far corner of the lawn, though, you can see a dark cloud hovering over one of the buildings. Impending storm, you think, though none of the people around seem to be seeking cover.

You are crossing the space on one of the paths that bisect the grass, leading toward that far corner. When you reach the building presiding over that edge, the cloud remains above it. It hasn't loosed any rain yet but looks like it threatens to do so any second. A man is exiting the building. He is walking toward you. You keep walking, aiming for the gap through which the path slips between the buildings and beyond which you can see the city rising up again.

The man is still walking toward you, on track to intercept you before you can reach the road. As he draws nearer he says, Gita!, which brings you to a stop. He catches up to you and smiles, showing all his teeth. His thinning hair is oiled, and he looks older than most of the other people you've seen, perhaps a teacher of some sort.

I'm glad I caught you, he says. I wanted to talk to you about your most recent paper, if you have a moment. My office is just in there.

No, you say, you're mistaken. I'm not Gita.

His face reads anger for a moment until he resets his smile. You can feel goosebumps rising on your skin. Your hair prickles at the nape of your neck.

Gita, he says, what are you talking about?

He reaches a hand out to touch the flower in your hair and you flinch away, instinctively. That flash of anger, again. His cologne is overpowering, it has created its own sickly atmosphere around you. Your stomach is churning. You turn to walk around him and away.

As you do so, he grabs your arm. Let go of me, you say, trying to shake him off. His fingers dig deeper. You say it again, louder now. It begins to rain, sheets of water, droplets so close you can barely see through them. The water is everywhere, surrounding you. You feel like you are drowning, again, a third time. The feeling kicks up inside you—that urgent desire to swim, to live. You flail and kick and punch. You sweep your elbows and knees. You reach with your hands until you can grasp a wave that will deliver you to the shore.

And when you open your eyes you are standing on the road you were trying to reach just now. The sky is cloudless. You are dry like the storm never happened. You have the feeling of having vanquished a demon. You turn and behind you, the Gothic buildings are gone, the rest of the city filling that space, hundreds of anonymous faces filling the city, filling the space. The man you just encountered has evaporated.

A few blocks farther and you are back at the beach, the sea. It's growing dark and the lighthouse flicks on, the beam plying the settling dusk.

How will I get home? you think. But in the time it takes to think this, you are there.

Your sea, again. It's dusk here, too, and dangerous to be out on the cliffs at night. The wind is picking up, screaming through the gorse. You hasten into a jog and then a sprint, flying back down the trail until you reach your house. You burst in the front door and find your mother sitting in front of the wall of windows, looking at the sea.

Where have you been? she asks. You are surprised to see concern on her face. You did not think your mother kept track of your comings and goings. The concern gives you pause. It makes you think (I) you should tell her everything and (II) you definitely shouldn't.

Just walking, you say. I was out on the trail near the lighthouse.

Just walking? she repeats. For three days?

Oh shit, you think. You feel like the house might collapse around you. Like you might, because time has already.

Your mind is not moving fast enough to craft a convincing excuse. You aren't sure there is one she'd believe. You have no friends around here you might have gone to see, no errand that might last for several days. Nothing that would take you away from the house for an extended period of time without telling her.

Now you are left with the truth.

I found something, you say, while I was walking. You are not sure how she will react, but you forge ahead. I'm not sure how to explain it, you say, but it was an opening that took me elsewhere. To a city by another sea. I was walking around there, and it only seemed like a few hours before I came back here.

Your mother is looking at you strangely. What are you talking about? she says. That made-up story is the explanation you're going to give?

I told you I can't really explain it, you say. But it's what happened. Anyway, where else would I have gone? Doesn't this make as much sense as me having gone anywhere else?

No, she says. It doesn't. You can't just run off for days and then tell me nonsense.

She walks over to her office. She doesn't slam the door. Your mother doesn't really show anger, rarely raises her voice; she prefers the silent treatment. Silence is much more effective.

You sit in a chair by the window, watching your sea, wondering what more to tell her.

A day passes like this, and then another. You pass your mother in the hallways and in the kitchen and she looks at you, eyebrows raised, prompting you to say something. When you start the same story she holds her hand up to stop you. No, she says. Still that? Fine then. She goes back into her office.

As the days go on, you feel yourself growing less convincing. You are less convinced. But then you stand before the wall of windows at night and look at your own reflection, which seems different somehow. Your eyes glint like knives sharpened in another century that have yet to draw blood.

Your mother must notice too. You feel her eyes drifting over your face whenever she sees you, trying to find a place to anchor themselves.

During this time, you avoid the trail. You have the sense of having touched something you were never meant to. You feel you have come to understand something about your mother but it has not brought you closer; now you are (I) unrecognizable to each other and (II) too familiar to bear. Who are you now with this knowledge? Who now is she?

One day your mother startles you in the kitchen as you are making her toast with marmalade.

Who are you? she asks. You now see a glimmer of fear in her eyes.

Ma, you say, come on. Can we please end this? It's gone on long enough.

I'm serious, she says. Who are you?

Okay, you say. Your daughter, obviously.

No, she says. You look like her, but you're not. What have you done with her?

It's me, you say, what do you mean I'm not?

But your mother is backing away, back to her office. She shuts the door and you bring your hands to your face, feel your features. You think your mother is losing it but you go look in a mirror anyway. There you are, still you.

You feel yourself losing track of time. Days more and perhaps weeks must be passing. You and your mother are still barely speaking. A morning comes when you enter her office with a plate of strawberries. She looks at you and you see zero trace of recognition on her face. The cocoon is closing. You begin to feel afraid. You think you should take her to the doctor. She is young but perhaps her memory is failing, perhaps there is something eating away at her brain in the silence that you need to catch early, before it does more damage.

What will bring her back to you? You think again about the truth, which you'd tried so many times to tell her. You feel stupid when it dawns on you that you never tried to show her. You had been too engrossed in your own desire to return and also never to do so.

Today, you'll show her.

Through the windows, the bright sun paints the waves white.

Shall we go for a walk, Ma?

I'm not going anywhere with you, she says. I don't know who you are or why you're here.

Okay, you say, exasperated. You're right. I'm not your daughter. But I'd like to show you something. Something that will maybe explain everything. Will you please come with me?

You can tell her curiosity is piqued. She follows you out and pauses in the kitchen to wash her hands. She says yes, she'll come. Still, you see her slip a butter knife from the sink into her pocket when she thinks you're not looking. For some reason you find this endearing, her belief that she could wield a dull blade as a form of protection.

She grabs her jacket from the hooks by the door and motions for you to go out first.

You lead her out into the midmorning shine, the sky blue and cloudless above. The day is more glorious than you've had in months, but the trail is uncharacteristically empty. Your mother walks a couple paces behind you; you can feel her stare boring into the back of your skull. You pass the lighthouse, still in its usual location, the rain having washed out earlier attempts to move it. Onward you go, scanning the yellow gorse to the left for a hint of orange, those planted marigolds.

All the way here you'd harbored a deep-seated worry, welcoming the silence your mother left you in as it allowed you to brood. Would the pool and flowers still be here? Had you, in fact, imagined everything?

But there, finally, you spot it in the same place you'd remembered. Close to the cliff's edge, the pool placid and mirroring the sky. A flower has replaced the one you'd plucked, the circle complete once more.

Here, Ma, this is what I wanted to show you, you say.

Your mother is looking into the pool, studying her reflection. She seems to be deciding something. You pick two flowers and keep one, hand the other to your mother. She accepts it and puts it into her pocket, but leaves her hand in there, curled around the butter knife.

What am I looking at? she asks. What does this prove?

Just wait, you say. You'll see.

Both of you stand there for some time. The same worry returns, your stomach roiling with doubt, anxiety. Your mother is restless, fear rising until plainly evident on her face. The wind has picked up; it whips into both of your faces. You're almost thrown back by the force.

What have you done with her? she whispers at you. Is this where you buried her?

She's pulled the knife out of her pocket, brandishing it in your direction. You are scared, wondering how it's come to this. You are thinking of the familial contract: *you are the person I have always known you to be. Your self, already calcified when we first met.* You met your mother after her past. She met you before you knew of it. You will always have gained your childhood after your mother lost hers.

Unnatural, you think, to have retrieved what she left behind. And yet—you are also born of what made her.

Please, Ma, you say, please stop. Stop and look at me; you know it's me.

But she will not look at you. Her gaze is fixed somewhere below your face, focused on your clavicle. The first bone to ossify in an embryo. Your mother, who grew your bones inside her, who no longer recognizes what came from her body.

She is advancing toward you and you are backing away. The drop looms large behind you, the rocks jagged beneath. Please, you are saying. You are trying to reason with her, bring you both back into your bodies. You, mothering your mother.

But the wind is howling now, carrying away your words. One step farther and you will be like the pebbles you dropped from these edges, listening intently for a splash you could never hear. Is this where the portal meant to lead you? To the brink and then over?

No, you decide. There is no fate. There is only the web that binds each of you together with your choices.

A gust catches your mother off guard and she drops the butter knife, bends over to retrieve it. You see behind her that the pool is ascending, forming the shimmering, vertical surface you remember. The mirror, the door, the opening.

You rush past your mother toward it and she leaps up, hands empty, in surprise. She sees what's behind you and catches your eye, unsure. You regard each other, two unrecognizable people a thousand miles from whatever once moored you. Palms open, searching.

One step and you can be through the opening. Two steps and you both can be.

So do you:

(I) take her hand—or

(II) take her hand?

A Body More Than Flesh and Bone

I. HEART

The dogs know first, their high-pitched keening echoing off the stone walls marking the outskirts of the nearby town. A chorus of strays proceeds up the dirt path to the site and settles in a semicircle framing Anika's ankles. Shoo, she says halfheartedly. The nearest dog cocks its head and regards her quizzically, sensing her ambivalence.

Her hands are wrist deep in the red soil. The constant breeze covers everything with ochre dust—skin, clothes, nostrils—until she looks in her pocket mirror at the end of the day and wonders whether she, too, has been unearthed here. Her fingers reach for the solid object she previously brushed against. Larger than a pebble, firmer than a twig: the faint, chalky texture of bone.

She holds her hands still while her colleague, Carine, gently scoops out the surrounding dirt. Carine stops to smooth an errant black curl behind her ear and leaves a vivid smudge on her forehead. There is a reverent hush and a sharp intake of breath as the contents of the test pit become visible. The two women stare at three thin bones arrayed next to a clay tablet covered in unfamiliar script. The tablet lies to the left of the bones, near where a human heart would be if the rib cage were complete. The women hold their breaths deep in the closed fists of their chests. For several minutes no one, not even the dogs, makes a sound.

Do you know how to identify a ghost? Its feet are turned backward. Every few seconds we glanced at our toes, checking to see where they were pointed. Every night we dreamt we were walking in circles. Every morning we opened our eyes, expecting to see ourselves in [ ], the low valley of our birthplace. In other words, the beginning.

Anika agrees to a quiet celebration for the discovery, which means Carine cooks mutton biriyani instead of the usual chana dal. Initially, they took turns cooking, but after Anika's first charred dinner they both deemed the rotation needlessly punitive. Particularly since Carine sings while she cooks—old Hindi songs she learned from her mother, a famed Bollywood playback singer from the years when the lyrics read like secular hymns. Carine has a narrow nose and deep-set eyes, and she tells Anika that when she was younger, her parents called her *little bird*. As Anika files away her notes and equipment each evening, Carine's melancholy voice rings out like a nightingale's paean to dusk, keeping the two women company even as they go about their solitary close-of-day tasks.

They make quick work of the meal. Feeling generous, Anika flicks a piece of gristle at a dog salivating in the shadows behind her. Her own childhood dog— shaggy, loving, codependent—buried every bone offered to him instead of gnawing on a single one. The possibility of retrieval seemed incidental to him; he appeared far more interested in the fact that the bones had been saved, that he could roam the small plot of lawn under his watch knowing they were stored somewhere just beneath his paws.

Anika plucks a whole black clove out of the mound of rice on her plate and pockets it in her cheek, chewing it from time to time, allowing her tongue to approach a warm, familiar numbness. The copper serving pots and stainless-steel plates shine empty in the moonlight. That went quick, Carine says. When I went into the butcher's shop he laughed and said he and the grocer were betting on when the strange visitors would get sick of chickpeas.

Anika laughs. I wonder who won that bet, she says.

There is not much money or time for their project. No allowance for efficient ground-penetrating radars or radiocarbon dating facilities, or even meals outside the legume family. They have been granted only the briefest of grace periods to conduct an excavation by the most basic means of survey: eyes and hands and feet. In a way she finds their bare-bones setup its own form of grace.

There has to be more, Carine says. Right? She collects the plates and serving vessels, producing a metallic clamor that sends the dogs into the shadows. Anika nods, follows Carine to the makeshift sink. She hadn't even considered that the tablet they'd unearthed could be the extent of the find.

If you're buried with a text rather than under it, Anika says, it usually tells a story longer than *here lies X*.

Manifestos, maybe? Last wills and testaments?

Proof of life or lives, Anika muses. She scrubs at a stubborn crust of rice coating the bottom of a pot until it dislodges. In their field, initial evidence of human habitation almost always led to more. Whole cities had been uncovered after a child tripped over a single shard of pottery protruding from the soil.

Later, we were reborn, but so was the world. We used our tongues to create it. The river doesn't have to be a river, we said; the rock doesn't have to be a rock. The womb is a birthplace. The heart is nothing but a necessary organ.

Sati was punishment for living, for living beyond a hus-band, for a body cannot outlive its master. But we are still living—so what can we call life but a boon, the unexpected compensation for each of our inevitable deaths?

After Carine goes to bed, Anika stays by the fire's faintly smoldering embers. She thinks about how days like this seem to shift time. How the days leading up to today had felt interminable. She'd first seen the newspaper article two years ago, a tiny item buried on a back page: *Pipeline Extension Halted Due to Discovery of Human Remains.* On reading this she felt a tingling in the back of her skull, like a voice clearing its throat to speak. Her parents had long ago taught her to fear any detour off a prescribed path, so she resolved not to hear the voice. But it remained insistent, amassing force like a gradual change in weather—the faint inkling of a thunderstorm, clouds gathering in audience for a reckoning.

A truth is undeniable and time inexorable, Anika's grandmother used to say, though not in so many words. One morning Anika woke up in a desolate spot on the Deccan Plateau, just fifty miles from where her mater-nal grandmother had been born. Where there should have been no bones, where nearly everyone was cremated. She found she'd taken all the necessary steps to get there, down to securing a sabbatical and enlisting Carine to help with her strange, half-formed project. All because when she finally silenced the competing clamor, the voice had said only: *listen.*

II. JAW

In the space of a week, Anika and Carine discover five more clay tablets and dozens of skeletal shards. An abandoned yellow bulldozer observes their excavations from several hundred feet away. They remain acutely aware of its presence, extracting objects from the earth gingerly, as if straight from its rusted jaws. Somewhere, in the distant headquarters of a multinational construction company, there must be a boardroom full of men that want desperately for the bulldozer to continue its unearthing—to put something in the soil rather than take anything out of it—and this only spurs Anika and Carine's efforts. Their muscles ache from hours spent crouching over the ground, sifting dust in cordoned-off quadrants again and again to be sure they haven't missed anything. In the evenings Carine retrieves the jar of Amrutanjan that lives in the bottom of her purse, and they slather it on each other's backs. Heading to bed with the smell of menthol thick in her nostrils, Anika isn't sure whether it's the balm or the prospect of sleep that provides her the welcome sense of relief.

When they're confident they've fine-tooth-combed the entire area, they lay out the findings, sit and whisper over them as if expecting the slow roil of a diamond birthing itself from coal. Displayed on a table covered with Carine's linen scarf, the array looks like an exhibit in a natural history museum—a collection of fragments awaiting the correct syntax, a lengthy placard spelling out significance. Anika feels strongly that any reconstruction amounts to an educated guess, that for this, patience is required. She is attempting to form a bone-deep sense of the place, somewhere between intuition and premonition, where she assumes the voice speaks from.

Carine goes over to the table, gently touches each of the tablets. Heart, she says, almost inaudibly. Then jaw, then pelvis—

Where we found them? Anika says, catching on.

We need some way to refer to each of them. You finally going to use that extra linguistics degree?

In the beginning, the priests told us of [ ], who so loved [ ] that after he died she threw herself onto his funeral pyre. The gods cut her body into fifty-two pieces, as if this might minimize the impact of her untimely demise. She was scattered over the earth: her left breast near [ ], her toe in [ ], her ringlets of hair near [ ], her wrists near [ ]. Later, we drank from a churning river and traced its source to a tranquil, green hollow. No one told us this was where her womb fell, but we recognized the place immediately.

In the afternoons Anika studies the tablets while Carine examines the bones. When Anika takes a break, she tries to help her friend work: measuring and remeasuring circumferences, comparing lengths and scribbling corresponding numbers in a thick, leather-bound notebook. Catching Carine murmuring calculations like incantations, Anika is reminded of how she first met her, in the antiquities wing of a museum attached to the university they both attended. In the museum she had slowly approached Carine, who was dressed in a close-tailored yellow kurta and whose curls were tied back in a headband that looked to be made of a zari border snipped off a sari. She envied the ease with which Carine wore her background; Anika had been trying for years to cover herself up, never acknowledging the futility of this effort. Carine was looking intently at a broken portion of a hammered gold necklace. When Anika stood next to her, Carine said, unprompted: this belonged to that woman over there, pointing to an unrelated partial skeleton in the corner of the room. She offered no explanation, but said it with such certainty that Anika didn't ask how she knew this. When Anika came back a week later, she understood that the lines of the necklace matched the shape of the skeleton's collarbone exactly. She remembered being surprised, once she saw it, that no one else had noticed it before.

Even across the dimly lit hall, Anika had recognized Carine as kin. She was relieved, over the years of their friendship, to find that they shared much more in common than the same shade of brown skin and black hair in a familiar milieu of no-one-else-who-looked-like-them. On first glimpsing Carine, Anika understood what must have been the swelling of relief in her own parents' bellies whenever they spotted a fellow Indian in their majority-white suburb: the solace in finding a single other face that affirms that you are not an anomaly.

The tablets they found are all inscribed in a fluid, unknown script. Whereas Sanskrit script is tethered to a flat bar, this one is unmoored, rolling across the page in a loose, sinuous scrawl. Anika searches for hours online—enduring the site's spotty, painfully slow connection—but cannot locate a single reference to such a language. She falls down an infinite number of internet rabbit holes, but none leads to the text she is holding in her hands.

And in her palms, usually slick with sweat but now bone-dry: a pound of clay crawling with calligraphy, words to be stared at, words to be stared at long enough to be understood. If you stare at a thing long enough, you begin to notice patterns. Perhaps you invent or impose patterns, dream a palace out of ruins.

Years ago, on a trip to the Acropolis—feeling out the first contours of a future career—Anika had been asked by a harried father where he could find a particular forum labeled on his map. Anika had been sitting on a bench sketching that exact structure, as it had once looked, superimposed on the current landscape. You're standing on it, she said. The man scanned the space around him, a wide field with a few column-stumps peeking through the sea of tall grass studded with blood-red poppies, then glanced pointedly at her sketch. You have to use your imagination, she added, seeing the man's evident confusion, his rising disappointment. He walked away with his two bored, earbudded teenagers, shaking his head.

Laid out side by side on her cheap folding table, the tablets form an uncharted, self-contained topography. For several days Anika merely lives with them, the tablets lurking in the wings of her vision, gaining the hushed intimacy of an underwater landscape. Then she grabs thin paper and wax crayons, and ever so carefully, as if she is making a gravestone rubbing, transfers the etched text on each tablet to a new sheet. She traces the script over and over, until she has to make new rubbings because she's ripped straight through the paper. On the third transfer, she realizes the peripheral drawings she took for decoration are a key. The shapes she's tracing resolve themselves into letters, words and phrases. She learns to distinguish the blank spaces indicating the end of a sentence from a proper noun omitted, intentionally, for anonymity; she comes to understand that both pauses signify, in their own way, a quiet desire to continue.

When enough of the strokes are identifiable, she attempts to speak the language aloud. Without meaning to, she falls into the flat cadences of English, her own native tongue. But the words seem to want to be chanted; they crave elision and lilt.

To build the world we summoned [ ], the goddess of speech. In the beginning, they told us she was a cosmic sound, a muse that inspired men to write inspired texts. They said she created the sacred language. But we listened more carefully: we understood that she was not the energy but the words; she was a hymn only we could hear. Our fingers described the sounds and inscribed them in shapes the men never could have imagined. Yes, we wrote everything down, what happened to us, the beginning, the end, no seamless transition between the two. But do not call us the authors of this history. We were a vessel for an ancient voice; we spoke the true names of what had always existed.

The red numbers on Anika's battery-powered alarm clock flip over to 0:00. The first pattering of rain, the dull plopping of droplets against canvas. The rhythm of the shower picks up and she recites the words on the tablets again, matching the swelling intensity. The words no longer seem to catch in her throat; they flow, unencumbered. She admires the way the texts are strung together—a new vocabulary pieced together from an ancient one, freed from the constraints of rigid grammatical structure. She begins to write out her translations, piecing together a story of the tablet authors' beginning and ending, a before and after for their creation of the language.

As the deluge peters out she sinks—wrung out, breathless—to the threadbare rug that serves as the floor of her tent. She hears, suddenly, a loud yell from Carine's tent. Anika runs out in bare feet, forgetting that the uneven ground will be littered with puddles. Inside her tent, Carine is hopping around as if the ground is strewn with flaming coals. When she sees Anika's face emerging between the canvas flaps, she freezes.

I figured it out, they each say in unison.

The bones, Carine says. I heard you muttering in your tent earlier about the tablets and it made me think of the jawbone. I remeasured. From the size, it definitely came from a woman.

Well, Anika says. I finally deciphered the tablets. You'll want to hear what was written there.

Carine continues remeasuring while listening to Anika's translations. She confirms what Anika already suspects: every one of the bones they've found belonged to a woman.

III. SHIN

A period of hot winds comes like an airborne plague of stinging nettles. Anika and Carine tie handkerchiefs around the lower halves of their faces while they work, tightly zipped in either one of their tents. To pass the time they aren't immersed in the tablet women's world, they take to pretending they live in another, as in: what if we excavated our current civilization ten thousand years in the future; what if we had the power to change a single event of the historical past; what if we were the last two people on Earth and left nothing behind; what if all we left behind was entrusted into the hands of other people.

I wonder how long we'll have to hide out here, Anika says, starting the game.

Until that railroad baron makes enough money to forget about the crores we took. So, like ten more minutes.

Anika giggles. What then?

We go to the market. Find any women picking out coins from their palms like each coin has to count. Slip a thick wad of rupees in all of their purses. Disappear into the hills.

Will they write songs about our names? Are we infamous?

Nah, Carine says. In deed only.

Better that way. Only one of us could give the songs their due anyway.

Maybe you can sing in this universe, Carine says. In fact, maybe you learned to from the birds that bring us news of all the earth's other creatures. So how long should I tell the birds we're staying here? she says, restarting.

I hope forever, Anika responds. It's quieter than any place I've ever been.

She means quiet in the sense of peaceful, because there is never any shortage of noise—dogs barking, truck horns from the distant road, various insects playing their legs like string instruments. She means that when dark falls, the lull takes the shape of a gently rocking cradle, and when the sun rises, a single yawn can soften the lengthening shadows.

Over dinner Anika and Carine point their headlamps at the objects around them and call out their names in the tablet women's language. The words are rapidly becoming second nature. Anika is reminded of the annual visits she made to her grandmother's flat in childhood, its light-filled rooms echoing with the headlong sound of Telugu. While there, the language came easily to her, though she'd never learned it. She understood large portions of conversations and answered tentatively but correctly when spoken to. Still, her grandmother always looked at her sadly when it came time for Anika to go home to her parents.

You'll forget all about this when you leave, she said. And indeed, back in the effortless embrace of English, Anika had no desire to use different names for things, and her parents never forced her; the shame of losing a language remained an unspoken but necessary sacrifice between them. Yet Anika suspected that the roots of the words remained somehow embedded in her. How else did they so easily sprout when she returned to the light-filled flat, her own voice blending comfortably into her relatives' chorus?

The physical landscape of the area has shifted dramatically in the centuries since the runaway widows set up their collective in this space. Mountains have been whittled into plateaus, coursing rivers reduced to trickling streams, a fertile hollow dried out into an arid, bouldered plain. Anika and Carine call out the words for pots and rocks and a few scattered trees, sweeping the site in concentric circles of naming until at last they come to the embers by their feet. There is no word for fire in the tablet women's language—not since, they've surmised, those widows escaped sati and fashioned a new world from the ashes of a ritual burning.

In the beginning, the men told us stories of how [ ] tried to seduce [ ] with her beauty. But he resisted, so she turned instead to religious austerity. She fasted and starved; she meditated in icy pools and froze nearly to death; she slept and hardened herself to the unforgiving mountain. After years a priest approached and asked why she had destroyed her once-lovely body with such deprivation. My love for [ ], she said. The priest scoffed. [ ]? he said. You did all this for that crazy hermit [ ]? What a terrible waste.

On the day the winds abruptly cease, a man arrives at the site. The cloud his jeep kicks up is similar to the ones that have been harassing the site for days. Anika recognizes the logo on the jeep as that of the small, European institute that provided her funding. She guesses the man is about her age, or possibly a few years younger. He is dressed as if ready to star in a film adaptation about field work in an academic discipline, wearing a shirt and pants covered in miniature pockets of questionable utility. Anika knows the man only from his online institute biography—she scanned every one in preparation for her grant application—and as a name copied on emails she sends with updates on her work. She notices he has grown a thick, reddish beard since his website headshot was taken.

The man walks directly to where Anika and Carine are standing, hands to their foreheads, shielding their eyes from the harsh midday sunlight. He offers a damp palm to both of them and introduces himself, explaining that he has been sent by the institute to oversee the project.

Though she hasn't checked her email for several days, Anika senses there will be no mention in there of Robert's impending arrival. She feels altogether unprepared to react to the situation, unprepared even for the long shadow his presence casts on the ground she and Carine have crawled over and scoured, inch by inch, for weeks. In lieu of a more considered response, she reverts to default politeness.

She leads Robert to the kitchen nook and hands him a plastic bottle of water from the loudly humming minifridge. The label on the bottle depicts a gilded Lakshmi, goddess of good fortune, her arms outstretched toward the pink cap. She asks Robert his research specialty though she already knows it from the short list of his publications available on the institute's website.

I'm an Ashtadhyayi expert, he says. That's a 2,600-year-old treatise on Sanskrit grammar, he adds, though more than a passing knowledge of this text was necessary for Anika to even enter her linguistics program. She remembers that the treatise's author, legend has it, was killed by a lion; beasts cared not for intellectual virtues, went the tale. She wants to ask Robert whether he believes this story to be true but senses he might not have a sense of humor about the subject.

Carine joins them as Robert finishes speaking, having probably stopped first to check the jeep for useful supplies. I don't understand, she says, continuing a conversation aloud that she has clearly been having with herself. She has pulled her hair loose and Anika feels, suddenly, how tightly her own braid is wound, how it pulls at her temples. We've already determined this language is a unique dialect created by women, for women.

Robert scratches an inflamed mosquito bite on the side of his neck. Anika wonders how he could have been bitten in the space of the few hours' air-conditioned drive from Hyderabad airport to the site. Yes, I am aware of that, he says. But I was the closest expert the institute had available, so they sent me.

He lobs his empty bottle into the trash bin, the plastic ringing against the metal with a finality that suggests an end to this particular subject. He asks them to show him the tablets. As Anika directs Robert to her tent, she sees that Carine's face has taken on a strange frown, her lips frozen around a word she cannot, for once, bring herself to say.

Not a waste, [ ] said to the priest, and he's not crazy, I love him. No matter what further harsh remarks the priest made, [ ] did not budge in her devotion. The priest transformed, then, into [ ], the beloved god, the object of her affection. You stayed true, he said, embracing her, and for this I must admit I love you too.

What were we to make of this story? By the time we reached the end, we learned we did not need to pass a test to become deserving.

That evening, Anika and Robert sit by the fire and pick at their food. The way they have seated themselves—diametrically opposed—is not conducive to conversation, but Robert still attempts occasional small talk. Anika silently curses Carine, who retreated to her tent once she presented them with dinner. After a particularly long lull, Robert excuses himself, saying he should call his wife and say goodnight to his kids. He walks over to the tent he set up a short distance away from Anika's and Carine's. Anika listens to the low murmur of his conversation, the individual words indistinguishable but the tone clearly warm and gentle. Now and then his voice erupts in eager laughter, and she has trouble reconciling this version of him with the serious-faced man she encountered earlier.

Later, in her own tent, sitting on a wobbly string cot, she thinks of how she hasn't called anyone since arriving. The only person she might have wanted to call would have been Carine. Perhaps her mother, also, but that woman's powers of observation are too keen for Anika to confront in her current state. How are you doing? her mother would say, and Anika would say fine, in a completely normal voice. Then her mother would say: you chose this, you know. You wanted to study the fruits of everyone else's posterity instead of creating your own. And then Anika would hear her own voice crack as she denied this and have to lie awake all night with that wavering.

IV. WRISTS

There is not much for them to do, Anika realizes, once Robert takes charge of the tablets. Following the dust storms, the sky clears to a cloudless, smogless blue, with a depth that seems capable of storing any number of secrets. The sun marches around the sky with a new sweltering swagger. Still, Robert remains holed up in his tent, giving no direction other than that the women should wait for him to get up to speed.

For Anika and Carine, waiting entails sitting on two squat boulders, drinking cup after cup of cardamom coffee and talking of the nameless widows as if they'd known them personally. Their heads incline towards each other when they speak, and they notice how their combined shadows form an unbroken wishbone. The pack of dogs assembles, tongues lolling, beneath a nearby neem tree offering a fat patch of shade.

You know, Carine says, all the bones are of average mortality-aged adults.

I know, Anika says, they must have lived here for years without ever being found. There is no need to add that she doubts anyone ever came looking.

On her first day of university, Anika's anthropology professor had opened his lecture by saying, portentously, that prehistory was 99 percent of the past. She understood, later, that he took the invention of writing as the great dividing line, that the desire to record was inextricably wrapped up in the recording. Over time Anika grew to agree: the bulk of the past seemed to lay long before the telling. At the very least, a long and buried detour outside the common telling.

In the beginning, we were not allowed literacy, but we were always watching, always listening. The priest told us many stories, but years passed before the words rearranged themselves into a moral we could put down in writing. For instance: one night [ ] was reciting scripture to his wife, but she fell asleep while he was reading. The god was enraged, and cursed her to be reborn a mortal. And so she was, as the most beautiful woman in a small coastal fishing village. After his wife was gone, the god found that he missed her terribly. So the god transformed his bull into a shark and sent it to terrorize the fishing village.

At mealtimes Robert emerges, squinting and rubbing his eyes. He offered to take over cooking upon arriving, but Carine refused, muttering that there wasn't much else for her to do otherwise. There are days Anika feels Carine could stew the chickpeas in simmering resentment alone. Though they eat together, conversation is sparse, and Robert never mentions the tablets or the project. She thinks it would be difficult for an outside observer to discern the relationship between the three of them; it is difficult, at times, for Anika to remember why she herself is there. She begins carrying her translations of the tablets in her pocket as a reminder, fingering the folded paper like a worry doll until it softens into a fabric-like consistency.

One afternoon, Robert receives a phone call in his tent. Just a minute, he says, and walks away from the camp until he is a khaki speck in the similarly colored landscape. He returns after fifteen minutes, making his way to where Anika and Carine are sitting by the fire, watching a pot of water until it gives in and boils.

Robert's face has turned a bright, purplish shade of red. His mouth opens and closes several times without words escaping his lips. Anika senses immediately that the news is bad.

Did you need something? Carine says, breaking the uncomfortable silence.

Oh, he says, looking up as if she had interrupted him. Well, that was the institute that just called. We discussed some thoughts on the—on the, uh, organization of this project.

Anika waits for him to continue until it's clear that he won't. Well? she says.

Well . . . we determined that the, uh, language is the significant discovery here. So that means—that necessitates that we no longer devote any resources to studying the human remains.

I'm sorry, Carine, he adds, but she has already gotten up and started walking to her tent. Anika stares at Robert's face, but he will not meet her eyes. He sits down next to her with a dramatic sigh and puts his head in his hands. Anika stands to go after Carine, but her feet do not follow. She feels paralyzed by the burden of expectation—Robert expecting some invective, Carine expecting more than platitudes. Her mind empties and she remains where she is standing. Carine is packing, and singing. It is a new melody that Anika has not heard before.

A logoed jeep arrives for Carine the next morning, and she leaves after an unemotional good-bye.

I'll see you back there, she says, though Anika is not sure yet where that would be.

She hopes Carine is heartened by the fact that Anika remains at the site, that from this, something may still be salvaged to make their work worthwhile. Their work has always been paramount; this principle had bonded them at university when it seemed any number of other competing demands might get in the way. As the jeep crawls toward the horizon, Anika thinks of how Carine had squared her shoulders before climbing into its passenger seat.

Robert avoids Anika for the rest of the day. He offers no further thoughts on the project or her status with it.

She sits in her tent, guessing the hour by the diminishing light and wondering if Robert, too, has left. Dinnertime comes and goes. Toward midnight, when her stomach's growls grow so insistent as to prevent sleeping, she nibbles at a rock-hard granola bar that she finds wedged between folders in her backpack. The mosquito coil in the corner has almost burned out, and the heady citronella fog in the tent makes her feel contemplative.

It has been hours, not days, since Carine left. Still, Anika feels the debt of borrowed time accruing, the anxiety brought on by uncertainty. She could be sitting in her tent for weeks waiting for Robert to receive another inevitable phone call, a comfortable space morphing gradually into a claustrophobic one.

Though the voice does not interject, Anika feels that it is present, angling for a particular decision.

The coastal villagers beseeched the gods for help, saying they would give the hand of [ ], their most beautiful maiden, to anyone who could rid the village of the menace. The god appeared after a few days, disguised as a fisherman and carrying the body of the dead shark over his shoulders. The villagers rejoiced. Here is your maiden, they said, and the god was grateful. For in reality, the villagers were returning his wife to him, whom he brought, happily, back to his mountain.

In the end, we understood the moral immediately: look what violence they wreak, to mend what they themselves have wrought.

The next evening Anika assembles her belongings. Everything still fits into the featherlight, nylon backpack she came with; she has accumulated nothing beyond stacks of paper, copious pages of notes and translations. And the bones and tablets, of course, though for these she feels a temporary guardianship rather than entitlement or ownership.

Outside, the sky has thrown down a carpet of black velvet and the new moon night feels like an auspicious sign. She changes into the one salwar kameez she packed, knowing she cannot show up suddenly in the nearby village in the shorts and T-shirts she wears daily at the site, no matter how local her face looks. The cotton top and pants give off a strong odor of camphor, one she associates with deep armoire shelves and rarely worn clothes. She ties the chiffon dupatta over her flashlight, lessening its beam into a hazy green glow.

Anika pauses at the entrance to Robert's tent until she hears the faint rumble of a snore. She unzips the opening one tooth at a time. The tablets are laid out on a plastic folding table identical to hers, set against one canvas wall of the tent, parallel to his cot. She makes sure Robert's eyes remain closed as she takes the tablets, one by one, and wraps them loosely in a jute bag that once held basmati rice. She tucks the bundle in the outer pocket of her backpack.

As she rezips the opening, she feels a pang of regret at leaving the bones behind. They are still in Carine's tent, lying naked on a similar folding table. There is the embodiment of the community, Carine would say; that these widows lived, that they once lived here.

But Anika knows she can't carry everything. It has to be enough, she thinks, to have only the body of words; it has to be enough to have left with the women's language. The final tooth of the zipper locks into place and Anika exhales with relief, her breath releasing, finally, at a volume just below a contented sigh.

V. PELVIS

Anika picks her way carefully along the path, worried about tripping but even more worried about stopping. She reaches the nearby village at about ten o'clock.

The owner of the grocery store is standing outside his darkened shop smoking a beedi. He recognizes Anika and smiles, motioning that he can reopen the shop if she needs. She shakes her head no and keeps walking, conscious suddenly of the hour, the empty streets.

She passes a tailoring shop with its lights still on. She can see several women inside, seated under glaring fluorescents, nimbly feeding material to chattering sewing machines. As she opens the door, an attached bell clangs loudly. The women all look up, expectantly. Anika tells them that she needs to leave the village, that she needs help. They point to the back of the room where a woman wearing reading glasses is seated at a solid teak desk, violently punching numbers into a calculator.

The head tailor turns out to have a daughter who attends college in the nearby city. She insists Anika stay with her until dawn, when the tailor's daughter leaves on her daily commute. Anika accompanies the woman back to her house, which is quiet but full with the breathing of sleeping bodies. Though it is late and Anika protests, the woman retrieves a plastic container of cauliflower curry from the fridge and heats it in the microwave. She pulls out a chair for Anika at the dining table, which is draped with a spotless white tablecloth embroidered with blue flowers. She brings her a cold glass of buttermilk and waits while she eats, not going to bed until Anika has wiped her plate clean with a third chapati.

In the end, we plucked the one harmonious chord in the universe and lived for years in its continued vibration. We hid ourselves in plain sight where we could not be found. They thought we would be dressed in white, forever condemned to half-life by [ ] and all the rest of the gods. But we clothed ourselves in all the colors of the earth, our bodies holied by our own sacred utterances, invisible only to those who stopped seeing us.

Anika wakes to what she assumes is the head tailor's daughter. In the weak light she can make out only a girl in her late teens, her eyes heavily lined with kohl. Time to go, the girl hisses, poking Anika's shoulder. By the way, I'm Parvati.

Parvati has a new-looking Bajaj scooter in a sickly shade of bubblegum pink. It boasts a sheen that can only be maintained with frequent washings, and Anika senses that to Parvati, the scooter represents more than a simple means of transport. Parvati hands Anika a helmet stickered with cartoon animals. My old one, she explains, as she fastens a plain black one under her own chin. She cautions Anika to hold tight, though Parvati turns out to be an exceedingly careful driver, following traffic laws though no one else around her appears to do so. As she weaves expertly onto a main street, into the growing rush of morning traffic, Anika loosens her hug around Parvati's waist but does not let go entirely.

Anika wonders whether she would ever so readily aid a complete stranger. What inspired such generosity, the kind that sped along like this, carefree, secure in the fact of its necessity, requiring no reciprocation? If she ever had her own daughter, Anika wonders whether this girl would be able to address the world with ease; whether the world might one day change and become easier for a girl to address. The streets blur to a rushing stream of colors, the sounds to a low-level hum. Anika ducks her head into the protected space behind Parvati's back and wonders, not for the first time, whether the future would ever become as readily imaginable for her as the past.

Several times at traffic lights Anika thinks she sees Robert—crossing the street, riding a motorcycle, sitting in an auto-rickshaw. But it is only a trick of the light, the sunlight reddening a beard at a certain angle. Nonetheless, each time it causes a fleeting rush of fear to pierce the bravery Anika feels she is wearing as armor. It takes time, the voice says, for steel to weld itself to bones; much longer for it to remain legible in your marrow, decades after your demise.

A few years earlier, Anika came across a retelling by Plato of a Socratic dialogue between two Egyptian gods, Thamus and Theuth, the latter the god of writing. In response to Theuth's exaltation of writing as a winning potion for humanity, Thamus argued that writing was dangerous, for it would slowly replace memory, rendering humans beholden to external texts that could speak only what had been written and thus give only an appearance of truth, lacking true wisdom. Anika remembers laughing upon reading this, imagining these men in a room speaking of truth as if they desired all forms of it to be preserved, speaking of dead texts as if they strained to hear the wisdom of the voices between or buried under the lines. What was memory, after all, but an act of memorialization; what was a person's existence—their experience, written down, unerased—but a truth in and of itself? So what if a truth from a dream was written down and called a memory, if memory lived through recurring dreams spoken as truth? The act of writing seemed its own form of wisdom—a vessel for both truth and memory, a future antidote against forgetting.

In the beginning, there was to be a burning. There were to be two bodies reduced to ash, one dead, one living. Instead, we are proof that there was a living: that there were no burnings so there would be something left for you to find. In the end, there were no children; there were only these lives, this tale, this desire for preservation. In the end, what else can this language say? Other than: listen; other than: hear all of this; other than: tell all of it, every word, to your children.

The outskirts of the city materialize after about twenty minutes. Buildings grow denser and taller until they become reef-like structures, layers upon layers arranged in a complex, resilient ecosystem.

That's my college, Parvati yells, pointing at what appears to be a storefront with a peeling sign on the second level of a building.

They continue on for several more minutes. Anika spots a board for the train station, and Parvati pulls into the entrance drive. She slows smoothly to a halt behind a line of idling Ambassador taxis.

Here you go, she says. Train station.

Anika pulls off her helmet and hands it to Parvati, who hangs it by its strap in the narrow crook of her elbow. Standing there, Anika feels like the words "thank you" are woefully insufficient, that there is much more she wishes to say. She asks if she can buy Parvati a cup of tea. Parvati checks her watch and, satisfied with the time she sees there, agrees.

Inside the station, still in the midst of awaking from its overnight slumber, there are pockets of concerted activity: a mustached man mopping up an unidentified liquid in a corner, a newsstand owner barking headlines, a uniformed railway agent sprinting toward a belching train, hat clutched in his hand. The departures board reanimates at regular intervals, clicking out delays and platform numbers. She watches it for several minutes, and hears the voice say a word that seems to mean both *go* and *stay* at once.

She buys a one-way ticket with a stack of her remaining rupees, and a chai for Parvati, admiring the practiced way the chaiwalla threads the liquid in a thin strand between two steel cups to cool it. On a whim, she buys a Thums Up for herself, having not had the soda for years, decades even. The first sip tastes exactly as she remembers, a sweet and heavily carbonated artifact of childhood straight from her grandmother's flat.

When she returns outside, Parvati is waiting in the exact spot Anika left her, leaning protectively against her scooter. The city grit and smog has already clouded the scooter's careful detailing, but the pink still draws the eye immediately, like a beacon. Parvati is carefully scanning the faces in the unbroken stream of people coming out of the station's entrance. As she spots Anika she smiles, her face alight with recognition.

Credits

Gratitude to the following publications, where some of these stories were previously published in slightly different form:

"Come Tomorrow" in *Salamander* (2024)

"Empires Have Been Destroyed" in *Witness* (2020)

"A Working Theory of Optical Illusions" in *Cream City Review* (2020)

"Bloom" in *The Rumpus* (2022)

"Pillow Book of the Dead Prince's Intended" in *Sonora Review* (2019)

"A Body More Than Flesh and Bone" in *The Offing* (2019)